timeless

LARK COVE SERIES

USA TODAY BESTSELLING AUTHOR

DEVNEY PERRY

TIMELESS

ISBN: 978-1-957376-17-2

This is a work of fiction. Names, characters, places and incidents are the product of the author's imagination or are used fictitiously. Any resemblance to actual events, locales or persons, living or dead, is coincidental.

Editing & Proofreading:
Elizabeth Nover, Razor Sharp Editing
Julie Deaton, Deaton Author Services
Judy Zweifel, Judy's Proofreading

Cover: Sarah Hansen © Okay Creations

Formatting: Stacey Blake, Champagne Book Design

timeless

prologue

CHARLIE

I LOOKED LIKE DEATH.

Red-rimmed, bloodshot eyes. Snotty nose. Splotchy cheeks. I had that weird saliva thing happening where I opened my mouth and a spit string stretched between my top and bottom lip.

"Attractive, Charlotte." A fresh wave of tears flooded until my gaze was so blurry that I couldn't see my face in the bathroom mirror.

No one called me Charlotte. Not since I was a little girl. Because—according to Mom—at the age of four, I'd declared I hated the name Charlotte.

Hate was a bit extreme. I didn't loathe my name. I just preferred Charlie. I had since the day a boy at the local camp in my hometown of Lark Cove, Montana, had called me Charlie.

"What was his name?" I asked myself in the mirror. Roy? Ray? Maybe Mom remembered. It had been too long, and my mind wasn't the sharpest today.

Regardless of that boy's name, no one in my life called me Charlotte.

Except Dustin.

He'd called me Charlotte from our first date to our last. Until the day he'd broken my heart. Even as he'd been frantically zipping up his jeans and begging for the chance to explain why his dick had been inside another woman, he'd called me Charlotte.

Charlie fit me better than Charlotte. My nickname was as comfortable as the boyfriend jeans and vintage tee I'd pulled on this morning. I preferred tennis shoes to heels. Cold beer to fancy cocktails. My hair hadn't been trimmed in months and my makeup routine took less than three minutes.

At least when I cried, there wasn't much to cry off besides the mascara that was now smudged beneath my eyelashes.

"Bastard," I muttered, wiping furiously to dry my face. "Ugh."

Dustin didn't deserve my tears. That's what Mom said. So why couldn't I get them to stop?

"Charlie." Dad's voice sounded from outside the bathroom door as his knuckles rapped on the wood. "We're going out on the boat. Want to come?"

"Go without me," I called.

"You sure?"

"Yeah." My voice cracked.

"Okay." He paused. "I love you, peanut."

"I love you too, Dad." My chin quivered as he lingered in the hallway. Like a silent hug. Dad had been hovering close since the Dustin disaster.

After a few long moments, his footsteps retreated, probably to round up Collin and Camila.

Before I'd escaped to the bathroom for yet another cry fest, my younger brother and sister had been running around with my cousins in the yard.

My aunt Aubrey and uncle Landon were visiting from New York with their two boys, Greyson and Bodie. Our whole extended family had congregated in Lark Cove for a week together.

This was my first trip home in months. I should be laughing and happy, soaking up every minute with the people I loved most, not blubbering every hour, on the hour.

"You suck, Dustin Lewis." He was ruining my vacation.

My plan was to spend the week in Lark Cove before heading back to Bozeman for a job interview. I'd just graduated from Montana State last month with my business marketing degree. My senior year I'd interned with a tech startup, and my supervisor was hoping I'd take a vacant business analyst position. The interview was for show—the job was mine if I wanted it.

Did I want it? It certainly wasn't my dream job, not that I had a dream job in mind. At this point, I simply wanted to be employed. And up until yesterday, I'd wanted to be employed in Bozeman.

For Dustin.

He'd graduated from MSU a year ago and had been working for his dad's cabinet company. I'd designed my entire future around his because he had no plans for leaving Bozeman.

What now?

In less than twenty-four hours, I'd lost my boyfriend, my home and my cat.

Why hadn't I listened to my parents when they'd offered to buy me a house in Bozeman for college? I'd insisted on having a *normal* college experience. To forge my own path and earn my own money, like Mom had done when she'd been my age.

My freshman year I'd lived in the dorms. My sophomore and junior years, home had been a cheap rental with two friends. Then this past year, Dustin had asked me to move in to his place.

Two years together and it was over. Done. Destroyed.

Dustin had been swamped at work lately, too busy to come to Lark Cove this week. Knowing I wouldn't see him for a while, I'd stopped by the shop yesterday to bring him lunch. But rather than find him buried in paperwork, I'd found him buried in his dad's assistant.

The saddest part of this entire ordeal was that it had taken me no time at all to pack my things. To pack up the life I'd thought Dustin and I had been starting.

Hours, just hours, after I'd found him fucking that woman, my SUV had been stuffed with my belongings, and I'd been speeding down the interstate.

Why hadn't I grabbed the cat? Loki had been Dustin's pet, not mine. But the cat liked me more.

I missed my cat.

Feet thudded outside the bathroom, followed by giggles. Then a door slammed and the house went still.

I sighed and grabbed a wad of toilet paper, blowing my nose. I dried my eyes one last time and opened the door, emerging into the hallway.

The sound of distant laughter drew me toward the long wall of windows at the back of the house. Beyond the glass, the sun shone brightly from the clear blue sky. Its rays caught the ripples in the lake, making them shimmer like stars.

As I opened the sliding door and stepped out onto the deck, the rev of a boat engine filled the air.

Dad was behind the wheel. Behind him was a cluster of smiling, laughing kids. Uncle Landon was untying the last of the ropes attached to the dock. Mom was standing in the bow, eyes aimed my way. She raised her arm in a wave, then blew me a kiss.

I blew one back.

Leaning my elbows on the deck's railing, I watched as Landon hopped in and Dad eased away from the dock, turning in a slow circle before pushing the throttle. The wakesurfing boat had every top-of-the-line feature available, including a ballast system and surround sound. He had three other boats on our private dock too, but that one was his new toy.

The engine thundered as they picked up speed, the sleek hull cutting a line in the water as they sped through the bay.

When they were out of sight, I dug my phone out of my pocket.

No texts. No missed calls. Not a word from Dustin.

For a man who'd promised to make it right, to win me back, to beg if needed, he'd been awfully quiet since I'd left yesterday.

"Asshole," I muttered.

"Yes. Yes, he is."

My head whipped over my shoulder as Aunt Aubrey stepped onto the deck. "Oh, hi. I thought I was alone."

"Do you want to be alone?"

Yes. No. "I don't want anyone to see me cry." It made Mom mad, and every time Dad spotted a tear, his eyebrows came together in this worried look.

"I don't care if you cry, Charlie." Aubrey's brown eyes softened.

"I know." I sighed as yet another wave of tears came crashing forward. "I just . . . ugh."

"His loss," she said, walking to a pair of chaise lounge chairs on the deck.

"Truth." I followed, taking a seat beside her and letting the afternoon sun dry my cheeks.

Aubrey gave me a smile before she plucked the sunglasses out of her hair and shielded her eyes.

People always said Aubrey and I looked alike. We had the same dark hair. The same nose. The same tilt to our upper lip. Aubrey was beautiful, inside and out, and other than Mom, if I had my pick of women to resemble, it would be her.

"I'm glad you're here." She patted my arm. "Even under the circumstances, it's so good to see you."

"It's good to see you too. And I'm glad to be home."

Lark Cove would always be home.

If there was any place in the world to mend a broken heart, it was here, in my hometown perched on the banks of Flathead Lake.

My parents' house stood proudly on the shoreline. The tall, pitched roof and plethora of windows provided a stunning view of this part of the lake. Surrounded by towering evergreens, it was a slice of paradise. The house itself was one of the most expensive houses in the area, but to me, it was simply home.

Despite my family's wealth, Mom had always worked hard to keep us grounded. Instead of hanging famous paintings, she'd put her own artwork on the walls. Her watercolors and oil canvases were mingled with photos of our family. The books on the shelves in the living room weren't there for decoration, but to read. Mom's and Dad's tattered paperbacks were mixed with young adult novels and our favorite children's books from when we'd been little.

The baseboards were scuffed from Collin's hoverboard. Camila had inherited Mom's artistic talents, and one night while she'd been painting in front of the TV, she'd dropped a blob of orange acrylic on the carpet. No matter how hard she'd scrubbed, the stain hadn't come out.

My room was the same as it had been before I'd moved out at eighteen, with mementos and knickknacks scattered on my own shelves. The dried corsage from senior prom. A birthday card from my gran, Hazel. The collection of cheap keychains that I'd picked up on family vacations around the world.

Mom's art studio, an old shed, sat beside the garage. And in the distance, nestled in a cluster of trees, was the fort I'd built as a kid. My hideaway from the world.

Hiding seemed like a good idea at the moment.

"Want to talk about it?" Aubrey asked.

"I don't know." My insides were a jumbled mess. Other than give Mom and Dad the dirty details, I'd spent most of my time since in tears. Maybe talking about it was the answer.

"I have all these questions," I said. "How did I not see it coming? How did I not know he was cheating? How long was he screwing around behind my back?"

In his rush of excuses yesterday, Dustin had promised it was a one-time lapse in judgment. He'd sworn it would never happen again. And he'd begged me not to tell anyone.

He'd begged me not to tell my family.

Maybe because he was worried they'd hate him forever. That he'd lose favor with Dad.

"Do you think he was with me because Dad is rich?" It was the question I hadn't been able to ask. Probably because deep down, I'd known the answer for two years.

Dustin had always been fascinated by my family's wealth, so much so that he'd done his capstone research project on the Kendrick Foundation, including an interview with Dad. When Aubrey had been on the cover of *Forbes* last year, he'd bought extra copies to give to his friends, making sure everyone knew that she was my aunt.

I'd dismissed it as normal, as a boyfriend taking an interest in his girlfriend's heritage. But maybe it had always been about the money.

"What do you think?" Aubrey asked.

"Yes," I admitted. "I think that was part of it."

"I wish I could tell you that every person you meet will look beyond the money."

But they wouldn't.

Aubrey didn't need to explain it. I'd seen it firsthand in college.

My father was the übersuccessful Logan Kendrick. Friends—or those who I'd thought were friends—treated me differently once they figured out who I was. Instead of splitting the check at a restaurant, they'd look to me to cover the bill. They'd ask to take my car wherever we drove because I could afford gas. I'd get invited to birthday parties for people I barely knew because they thought I'd bring a swanky gift.

Dustin had been different—or so I'd thought. He'd paid for our dates. He'd been the person to buy the expensive presents. When I'd insisted on covering half the rent, he'd hesitated until I'd pestered him long enough that he'd finally caved.

What if that had been a show, a way to worm his way into my father's life? What if the countless times he'd said *I love you* had been a lie?

What if all I'd meant to him was the promise of a future fortune?

Every unanswered question compounded the ache.

"Have you ever had a broken heart?" I asked Aubrey.

"Yes."

"What did you do to make it stop hurting?"

"There's nothing to do but give it time. The pain will pass. I promise." She shifted her gaze toward the lake.

Dad's boat zoomed across the other side of the bay. Behind it was the tube carrying Aubrey's two boys. Dad cut a turn, forcing the tube across the wake. It bounced and skidded until it caught an edge and tipped to the side, sending its riders crashing into the water. Even at this distance, we could hear their laughter and cheers as they waited for the boat to pick them up.

Aubrey laughed. "They love it here."

I smiled toward my cousins, the first real smile today.

"It will find you when you need it," she said.

"What?"

"Love."

Nope. No, thanks. Single sounded like a damn good plan to me.

"Your heart will heal," she said.

"When?" Because God, it hurt.

Dustin had never been perfect, but he'd been mine. When I'd imagined the future, he'd been by my side. And now . . . maybe what hurt the most was that those dreams were gone. Erased like they'd never existed in the first place.

"I don't know, Charlie. But here's something your uncle Landon taught me. It will happen when it's supposed to happen. There's no clock." Aubrey touched the diamond on her wedding ring. "Love is timeless."

one

Aubrey

Nine years earlier . . .

"ASSHOLE." I SNIFFLED AND DABBED MY EYES WITH a tissue.

No more tears. Not only did Tristan not deserve them, but I'd spent thirty minutes on my makeup this morning and wouldn't ruin it at his expense.

I leaned closer to the bathroom mirror, inspecting my wet eyelashes. My mascara was clumped. *Damn.* The dark circles beneath my bloodshot eyes were showing through my concealer. Even with my makeup, I looked like death.

"Ugh." Fucking Tristan.

I cursed his name, but deep down, I couldn't place all the blame for this total emotional meltdown on his shoulders. Sleep deprivation. Stress. Loneliness. They were the underlying culprits here.

Yesterday had been packed with meetings, per usual. And like always, I'd fallen behind on emails. The urgent messages in my inbox hadn't been able to wait until morning, so after going home last night, I'd worked for a few hours until finally crawling into bed at one.

My personal trainer had arrived promptly at four thirty this morning. Workout complete, I'd gotten ready and made it to the office by six.

What a week. Was it Tuesday? No, Wednesday. The days were running together in a blur. Sleep. I needed sleep. I had no time for this little crying jag, so I opened the drawer beside the sink, plucked out my makeup bag and got to work fixing my face.

"Engaged. Already?" I scoffed as I swiped on a fresh coat of mascara.

Apparently Tristan hadn't been as devastated over our breakup as he'd feigned.

Time to swear off men.

Again.

My junior year in college I'd vowed to stay single until graduation after a humiliating ordeal in the school's gym with my personal trainer at the time. In my defense, he'd had this killer smile and abs for days. We'd hooked up a few times, and one Saturday night, we'd gotten adventurous. The custodian had caught us together in the empty weight room.

There were few moments more embarrassing than being caught on my knees with a dick in my mouth. The next day, after being fired for violating the gym's employee code of conduct, he'd broken it off via text.

So I'd sworn off men. I'd focused on my studies, and

honestly, I'd been happier with a singular goal in mind—graduating with honors. But after working for a few years, I'd lifted the man ban.

Failed relationship after failed relationship. They stacked together in a line of crashing dominoes.

I was thirty-five years old. It wasn't just the days or weeks blending together, but the years too. And here I was, wasting them crying over assholes.

No more men. That strategy had worked for me in college. Why not try it again? Besides, it wasn't like I had time to date. Where was I going to meet someone? The conference room?

Everyone who worked in this building worked for me. Most men I met outside these walls were intimidated by my success. I refused to stifle myself to appease a boyfriend's fragile ego.

So I was done. Effective immediately. As the CEO of a multibillion-dollar corporation, I'd concentrate on running this company.

Kendrick Enterprises never asked me to sacrifice my goals.

Kendrick Enterprises didn't bitch when I came home late.

Kendrick Enterprises wouldn't dump me for a friend of mine from high school after I'd introduced them at an art gallery.

"Tristan and Tiffany." I rolled my eyes and threw my makeup back in the drawer, slamming it closed. According to the Instagram photo that had sparked these tears, they were engaged. Tristan and I had broken up two months ago. "Sounds like a freaking sitcom."

I was in no position to judge their alliteration. Abel and Aubrey had sounded just as disgustingly cute.

In the scope of my heartbreaks, Tristan's was merely a pinch. It stung that he'd moved on so quickly and with Tiffany, but in truth, he'd been my rebound from Abel.

Abel had been the man who'd delivered the real blows.

We'd broken up in January. It was October. Ten months later and I still thought about him too often. At least Tristan had offered a brief distraction.

Two ex-boyfriends in less than a year, and now both were engaged.

I'd held myself together when Abel's wedding invitation had arrived in this morning's mail. But when Tristan and Tiffany's photo had snuck its way into my social media feed, it had shoved me over the edge.

And here I was, crying in my corner office's private bathroom.

Over an engagement photo.

And a wedding invitation.

Why would Abel send me that invitation? To be spiteful? To rub it in my face? We'd dated for five months, and it had become fairly serious. In the end, he'd spent most nights at my penthouse, and I'd loved him.

Maybe. I wasn't so sure now.

Was the invite some sort of insult? He was getting married, so was this a reminder that I was still married to my job?

Newsflash: I was well aware of where I spent the majority of my time, and it was no insult. Something he should have always understood but couldn't seem to grasp.

Abel was a lawyer with a demanding career of his own. That had been the crux of our demise. Abel worked for the law firm that represented Kendrick Enterprises. Technically, I was his client.

Given the dynamics in play, the various contracts between the firm and my company, I hadn't wanted to make a big splash of our relationship. So we'd kept it secret. In the beginning, he'd agreed. But as time had passed, he'd grown more and more frustrated with my hesitation to make some grand announcement.

It was no one's business who was sharing my bed. People would ask questions and raise concerns about professional boundaries. I'd begged Abel to keep it a secret for just a bit longer. Instead, he'd called it off.

Was it me? Was I unlovable? Unmarriable?

My shoulders sagged as I stared in the mirror. Beyond the closed door, my phone rang.

Wallowing would have to wait.

I squared my shoulders and adjusted the lapels of my hunter-green blazer. I added another pin to the twist in my hair. I made sure the cream silk blouse beneath my jacket was tucked into my trousers, then walked out of the bathroom.

The heels of my four-inch Louis Vuitton booties clicked on the marble floor as I returned to my chair. In the ten minutes I'd been teary in the bathroom, my inbox had flooded.

I sighed, ignoring the emails to pick up my phone. A missed FaceTime notification from my brother. I tapped it, swiveling in my chair as the chime filled the room.

"Hey," Logan answered with a grin. "Busy?"

"Always." I smiled.

"We'll be fast." He glanced over his shoulder, then stretched out his arm, holding the phone farther away from his face. "Come here, Camila."

After a few seconds, a little face appeared on the screen as Logan picked up his daughter and set her on his lap.

My heartache instantly eased. "Hi, sweetie."

Camila smiled wider, putting her chubby fingers in her mouth as she snuggled deeper into Logan's chest. At three, my niece was as adorable as she was shy.

"We just wanted to say thank you for the gifts." Logan kissed his daughter's dark hair.

Camila's dark eyes danced as she stared into the screen.

"Can you say thank you?" he asked her.

"Fank you," she whispered with her hint of a lisp.

"You're welcome."

"Charlie and Collin say thanks too, but they're at school," Logan said. "That was very generous."

"If I can't be there in person to spoil them, then I'll do it from afar."

On Monday night, I'd been working late, alone with nothing but New York City's lights beyond my windows to keep me company. A picture of Logan's family was framed on my office bookshelves, and when I'd stood from my desk to stretch my legs, that photo had drawn my attention.

In the picture, Logan's wife, Thea, was tucked into his side, her hand pressed against his heart. And their three beautiful children were standing close. Five-year-old Collin had his head thrown back in laughter. Camila was hugging Thea's leg. And twelve-year-old Charlie was in the center, smiling wide.

Mom and Dad reminded us often how much I'd looked like Charlie at that age. It was uncanny.

As I'd stared at the photo on Monday, this black, endless hole had spread through my chest. So instead of returning emails for the rest of the night, I'd spent two hours online shopping, overnighting care packages of toys and books to Lark Cove, Montana.

It was hard living on the other side of the country and missing my nieces and nephew. But I tried to make up for it with regular calls. What was the point of being obscenely wealthy if you couldn't splurge on gifts for your favorite kids?

"Okay, we'll let you go," Logan said.

"Yeah, I'd better get back to work." I blew out a long breath. "Say hi to Thea for me."

"Will do."

"Bye, Camila." I gave her a finger wave, then ended the call, pulling up my calendar for the rest of the day.

Meeting after meeting. My only free window was for the next twenty minutes, so I picked up my desk phone, hitting my assistant's extension.

"Ms. Kendrick," she answered.

"I'm ready for you, Wynter."

"Be right there." She ended the call, no doubt to collect the stack of notes she'd created since our standing morning meeting.

Wynter loved sticky notes. Mostly I think she loved crumpling them up when she was finished with a task. So instead of electronic lists or a legal pad of tasks, she walked into my office with a fistful of neon-yellow Post-its.

"Okay." She took the chair across from my desk. She glanced up, her mouth open and ready to launch into her list—and paused, her eyes widening. "Oh. Are you all right?"

Damn. The phone's camera had disguised my red eyes from Logan, but with Wynter seated so close, there was no hiding the fact that I'd been crying. "Allergies."

"In October?"

I arched an eyebrow, nodding at her notes. "I have a meeting in twenty minutes."

"Sorry." She ducked her chin.

Wynter was a new member of Kendrick Enterprises. My former assistant, Gwen, had taken maternity leave three months ago, and after being at home with her baby, she'd decided not to return to work.

Gwen had been with me for five years. Replacing her had been agony.

Wynter and I were still fumbling through our routine. Getting to know one another. It wasn't that she was doing a bad job. Her methods were simply different, and she had yet to realize that I wasn't going to be her friend.

Making friends at work was impossible, something I'd learned early on in my career.

Friendships made firing an employee exponentially more difficult.

So I kept up boundaries. Employees, like Gwen and Wynter, called me Ms. Kendrick. Like they called my father Mr. Kendrick.

Wynter and I didn't gossip about interoffice relationships. We didn't go to lunch or talk about our favorite television shows. She could make friends with the other people in this building.

Dad had always warned me that being in charge was a lonely job. He wasn't wrong.

But at least I had my family. Logan, Thea and their kids. Maybe next weekend, I'd take a trip to Mom and

Dad's estate in Long Island for a change of scenery. And I had my sister, Sofia.

She was in Lark Cove too. She'd started seeing Dakota earlier this year, and from the sounds of it, their relationship was about to generate another wedding invitation in my drawer.

"Ms. Kendrick?" Wynter was staring at me, waiting.

"Sorry." I shook my head.

"Okay, so first. I have the mock-up for the article they're printing in *Entrepreneur* for your approval." She held out a folder, extending it across the desk.

I flipped open the folder and frowned.

The photographer who'd come here a few weeks ago had done a quick shoot in my office for the magazine's cover. He'd wanted something *authentic* to go with the article, and instead of taking photos at his studio, he'd come here.

I scanned the article, making sure there was nothing that needed to be changed. Dad had taught me a long time ago that the only interviews to take were those where we had copy approval.

We didn't do many interviews.

Especially after the mess Sofia had gotten into with a magazine earlier this year.

"Your publicist had a few notes," Wynter said, leaning forward to point toward the page. "They're in the margins."

I nodded, flipping to the next page. When I was

finished, I placed it on my desk and tapped the cover shot. "This is unacceptable."

The photo they'd chosen was of me standing at the windows behind my desk, appreciating the view that overlooked the city. My dark hair was down, artfully curled and draping over one shoulder. The dress I'd worn that day was black with three-quarter sleeves. The sweeping neckline had left my shoulders bare. A silver zipper stretched down my spine and to my ass.

But it was not a photo I'd posed for.

That damn photographer must have taken it when he'd lied and said he was setting up his lights. Another asshole.

"Tell them to find a different cover photo." I shoved the mock-up across the desk to Wynter.

"Of course."

Part of my job as a female CEO—the worst part—was proving myself to my male counterparts. Most would always consider me too young. To others, I was too pretty. No matter how many decisions I made for Kendrick Enterprises, no matter how much money we made, no matter what letters were stamped behind my name, there would always be a collection of men who wouldn't take me seriously because I was a woman.

This article in *Entrepreneur* was a flex. Not for the company. For me.

I wanted the men of this city to know that I was not to be ignored.

Sooner or later, Dad would be retiring. He'd already named me his successor. I was the acting CEO and, for all intents and purposes, the person in charge.

There was no way that I'd let these people feature *my ass* on this magazine. They could show my fucking face on the cover.

"What else?" I asked Wynter.

She started rifling through her notes, one yellow slip at a time, until all but three were crumpled in a ball.

A ding from my computer cut our meeting short, a reminder that I needed to be in the conference room down the hall in five minutes.

"See if you can find another window in my schedule this afternoon," I told Wynter, standing from my chair. "We'll finish up your notes."

"Thank you." She stood too, leading the way to the door.

I stepped into the foyer, ready to head to my meeting, but stopped. The receptionist, Leah, was rushing my way.

She held up a hand, signaling for me to wait. "Ms. Kendrick? There's a police officer here to see you."

"What? Why?"

Footsteps echoed through the open space. Behind Leah, a man in uniform strode our way.

My breath caught in my throat.

A muscular physique filled out the officer's uniform. His long legs ate up the distance between us as he strode my way, walking with that natural swagger that only truly confident and sexy men seemed to possess.

His dirty-blond hair was combed, but a little windblown. His chiseled jaw was sharp enough to cut a hole in my office windows with a single smile. And his crystal-blue eyes seemed to undress me with his every step.

This man wasn't just attractive, he was intoxicating. I couldn't tear my eyes away from that broad, strong frame. His badge gleamed beneath the overhead lights. His gun was holstered. Where were his handcuffs? Would they fit me? Would they fit around my headboard? Before I could will the image away, my cheeks flamed.

The corner of his mouth turned up in a cocky grin.

I pursed my mouth in a thin line, tapping my foot in an effort to appear annoyed. I crossed my arms over my chest, glad I'd worn a blazer today, because my nipples felt like pebbles inside my bra.

What was it about *him* that caused this instant, physical reaction? My body had reacted the same way on the day we'd met. At his police precinct.

"Officer McClellan."

That grin of his widened. "Hello, Aubrey."

two

Landon

"Hello, Aubrey."

"Ms. Kendrick," she corrected with a scowl.

No way in hell was I calling her Ms. Kendrick.

Not when using Aubrey seemed to ruffle her feathers. And what pretty feathers they were.

"What are you doing here, Officer McClellan?" She planted a hand on her hip.

"In the neighborhood. Thought I'd stop by."

I was here on a whim. I hadn't seen Aubrey in months, not since the day we'd met. But she'd been on my mind lately, and I'd been meaning to drop by but hadn't made the time. This afternoon, as I'd been walking back to the precinct after my lunch break, I'd passed by this building, the Kendrick name snagging my attention. I hadn't been sure if she'd even be here, but what the hell. I'd wanted to see her again.

Curiosity had finally gotten the best of me.

Aubrey cast a glance at the other two women hovering nearby, and with a single look, they scattered, leaving us alone. "Did you find my sister's Chanel?"

"Nope." Even when I'd told her repeatedly that her sister's handbag was lost, she hadn't listened.

This past summer, Sofia Kendrick had been mugged, and I'd been assigned to her case. Some asshole had stolen her purse and phone. She'd walked away unharmed, but that sort of violation was still rattling.

After collecting details to investigate and file a report, I'd done my best to comfort Sofia while being honest, explaining the likelihood that we'd find her belongings was slim to none. That designer handbag had probably been pawned less than an hour after it had been lifted. Same with her phone as soon as it had been wiped.

There were millions of decent people in New York City, but we had our fair share of pissants too.

Aubrey had been with Sofia after the mugging, listening as Sofia had given her statement. Then she'd thrown her sass in my face, asking questions about how I'd be handling the investigation and demanding justice.

I liked sass.

I liked sass a lot.

Muggings were unfortunate, and unfortunately, they happened too often. There wasn't enough manpower on the force to track down every petty thief.

But this was a woman who was used to getting her way. A woman who didn't take no for an answer.

Before leaving the precinct, Aubrey had given me her business card, her private number written on the bottom, so I could contact them until Sofia had found a replacement phone. I'd tucked that card in my uniform pocket and, later, slotted it into my wallet.

It was in my pocket at this very moment.

For some reason, I'd kept that card. Forgotten that card.

A mistake.

As she glared up at me, her lips pursed, I realized just how big of a mistake it had been to let Aubrey walk out of the precinct doors and forget.

"How have you been?" I asked.

"Fine." Aubrey tapped a foot on the marble floor, trying her best to appear annoyed. Except her cheeks were flushed. Her eyes kept darting to my mouth.

She'd definitely checked me out as I'd walked in, her gaze raking me from my hair to my boots. Hell, I'd done the same, appreciating every line of her dark green suit and the way it was tailored to her slender frame.

Damn, she was beautiful. I'd forgotten just how stunning she was, especially today, with her hair pulled back into a knot.

"Anything else, Officer McClellan? Shall we discuss the weather?" Aubrey raised her eyebrow, almost like she expected me to cower.

I didn't cower.

I smiled wider.

From her dark hair to those shoes that probably cost more than my entire wardrobe combined, Aubrey Kendrick was head-to-toe sass.

Yeah, I'd definitely made a mistake this summer.

I'd picked the wrong damn sister.

Because as Sofia and Aubrey had left the precinct, it had been Sofia I'd chased.

Obviously, I'd been fucking blind. Not that I regretted my time with Sofia. In the months since, she'd become a good friend.

Sofia and I had traded numbers after the mugging. I didn't give my personal number to just anyone, but she was so shaken up, I decided what the hell. The next day, even though it was my day off, I gave her a call. She'd already gotten a replacement phone, so I'd checked in to give her an update—that I had no update. She confessed to feeling creeped out and worried about going home. That the thief had stolen not only her wallet with her credit cards and driver's license, but also her keys.

So I offered to do a sweep of her penthouse apartment, make sure there wasn't a criminal hiding in her closet. After I swept her place, her personal chef made me the best cup of coffee in SoHo.

Before leaving, I asked her on a date. Sofia rejected me—then and every time after. Every time I asked her out for breakfast, lunch or dinner, I got a no. Maybe that was why I pursued her. That rejection.

I wasn't a man who was rejected often.

The only thing she agreed to was coffee on Sunday mornings.

So for two months, we met for coffee. Not exactly dates, but spending time with her was fun. We became friends, chatting about nothing serious. It was light. Entertaining.

Platonic.

Not once had I felt the urge to kiss her. To claim her.

Sofia Kendrick was a lovely woman, but she wasn't for me.

My ideal woman wasn't easygoing. She pushed and pulled and made me want to rip my hair out at times. She had a fire blazing in her gaze. She had a stubborn streak as wide as mine and an iron will.

My ideal woman was a challenge.

I needed a woman who'd keep me on my toes until those toes were in the grave.

It had actually been Sofia's suggestion that I give Aubrey a call. She'd planted an idea I'd been mulling over for far too long.

So here I was, finally, standing in front of this beautiful woman, wondering why the fuck I hadn't been standing here two months ago.

My body came alive as we stared at each other, my pulse quickening. This was the woman to kiss. To unravel.

My fingers itched to loosen that silky chocolate hair and wrap it in a fist.

Her nose was straight, the perfect line over soft lips.

Her mouth was painted a rosy pink, dark enough that it would leave a trace behind on my skin.

Christ, I was a fool. How could I have missed this spark?

"I'm late for a meeting." Aubrey's foot kept tapping. "Is there a reason for this surprise visit?"

"Oh, there's a reason."

"Which is?"

I smirked. "Think I'll keep that to myself for a bit."

"Excuse me?"

Those pretty brown eyes flared, pools so dark a man could drown. A storm raged in that gaze.

A storm that promised a challenge.

The challenge of my lifetime.

"Um, Ms. Kendrick?" The blond woman who'd come out of Aubrey's office earlier stood a few feet away, a hand held up.

So lost in Aubrey's eyes, I hadn't heard the woman approach.

Aubrey jerked, like she'd been snuck up on too. Her head whipped to the side and she straightened her shoulders, a vision of grace. A woman in her element.

She had this innate confidence and power, especially here, in a building with her last name on its face.

I remembered the sass from after the mugging, but I'd missed that air of command. Maybe because she'd been just as rattled as Sofia. Well, today it was as clear as the autumn sky. And sexy as hell.

"Yes?" she asked the blond.

"Should I tell them you'll be delayed for the meeting?"

"No." Aubrey frowned, looked up at me once more. "This has been . . . well, pointless."

I chuckled.

My laugh only seemed to piss her off. Excellent.

"You know the way out, Officer McClellan."

I didn't budge. "Landon."

With another scowl, she turned and marched past the blond, her heels a sharp click on the polished floor.

She was about ten feet away when her footsteps slowed, then stopped. She turned around, her chin held high, as she returned to where I was standing. But she didn't so much as spare me a glance as she ripped open her office's door and strode inside.

Aubrey walked straight for her desk, swiping up her phone. As she marched for the hallway, she refused to meet my gaze. But her cheeks were still flushed. It was only as she passed me by that she leveled me with another glare, a hint of floral perfume and lemon in her wake.

"Aubrey," I called.

She slowed, her frame tensing as she turned just enough to look at me over her shoulder.

"Good to see you." I winked.

She opened her mouth, like she was going to say something. Instead, she just huffed and disappeared around a corner.

Yeah, this was going to be fun.

I grinned.

"Is there anything I can help you with?" the blond asked.

"Nah. Thanks." I jerked up my chin, then made my way toward the elevators, in no rush.

I had a phone call to make.

But first, I'd let Aubrey get settled into her meeting.

The receptionist gave me a shy smile as I passed her desk. Stationed at her side was a hulk of a man wearing a black suit. Bodyguard? Probably.

I nodded to them both, then hit the button for the elevator. The doors opened instantly and I stepped inside, letting it whisk me to the first floor.

The security guards stationed at the front desk both nodded as I strode through the lobby. When I'd arrived earlier, I'd told them I had a private matter to discuss with Aubrey Kendrick—not entirely a lie—so they'd pointed me in the right direction, telling me to stop by her assistant's desk on the fortieth floor.

As I stepped through the revolving door and onto the sidewalk, the October chill seeped through my coat. I stuffed my hands into my pockets, glancing up at the structure towering overhead.

The Kendrick Enterprises building was located in Midtown. It wasn't as tall as some of the famous skyscrapers in the area, but it gleamed under the afternoon sun with windows stretching from the bottom floor to the top.

It was a building fit for a queen.

I smiled to myself as I strode down the block, pulling my phone from my pocket.

Today's visit had been a whim. The rest would be on purpose.

That spark was just too damn promising.

With any other woman, I'd lay it out there. Ask for a date. Dinner. Conversation. We'd get to know each other. Play it slow.

Not Aubrey.

I had no doubt that if I asked her out, she'd slam that door in my face.

So this time, I wasn't asking.

Mom had always called me a bulldozer. When I had my mind set on something, I made it happen. Like when I'd told her I wanted to follow in Dad's footsteps and become a cop.

I'd just finished my sophomore year of college and known there was no way I could gut out another two for my bachelor's degree. School was dull, and though my grades had been decent, my heart hadn't been in it.

Mom had known how much Dad had loved being a cop, but she was a mother. She'd done her best to convince me that a boring office job was the golden ticket. A job with little chance someone would try to shoot me during a shift.

But even though I hadn't chosen the path she'd preferred, there hadn't been anyone prouder when I'd finished with the academy. Mom had always been my biggest supporter, from the day I'd been born to the day she'd died two years ago.

Fucking cancer.

I slowed on the sidewalk, turning to cast another glance at the Kendrick building.

Mom would have liked Aubrey's spirit. Because before the sickness had stolen Mom's fire, she'd had it in spades. There was a reason I was so stubborn. I'd come by it honestly.

Lacy would like Aubrey too. Hopefully, they'd get the chance to meet one day.

I pulled my wallet from my pocket, digging out the business card I'd carried around for two months.

Two months.

Maybe I hadn't been as oblivious to Aubrey as I'd thought.

I entered her number, saving it first, then dialed.

She answered on the third ring, probably having had to excuse herself from her meeting first. "Aubrey Kendrick."

"It's Landon. Just wanted to give you my number."

Even over the noise of traffic, I could hear her molars grinding. "Officer McClellan, I gave you this number so you could give me updates on Sofia's case, not interrupt my workday."

I chuckled. "Your sister didn't tell you much about me, did she?"

"Is there a point to this phone call? Or is it like your visit? A waste of my time."

"Yeah, there's a point."

"Which is?"

"To give you my number. Call me anytime."

"I won't."

I smiled. "Take care, Aubrey."

"Ms. Kendrick," she snapped, then ended the call.

I tucked my phone away, whistling on my way back to the precinct.

Yeah, this was going to be fun.

three

Aubrey

"Back to the office, Ms. Kendrick?" Glen asked from the driver's seat.

"Please. Thank you."

He nodded, then pulled away from the curb.

Glen was the newest member of my staff. He'd been Sofia's driver, but now that she was in Montana, she didn't have much need for a chauffeur. The timing had worked well because my former driver had decided to retire, so when Sofia had left the city, I'd hired Glen.

Beside him in the front passenger seat of my Rolls-Royce Cullinan was my bodyguard, Wilson. At six six, his head nearly brushed the SUV's ceiling. His shoulders extended well beyond the edges of the seat. He looked cramped, but beyond buying a tank to drive around Manhattan, I doubted any vehicle I bought would be spacious enough.

The Cullinan was a recent purchase, an effort to accommodate Wilson. He'd been with me since the summer. After the mugging, per Dad's insistence, Sofia and I had both taken on personal security. Along with Glen, Sofia had ditched hers when she'd traded the city for Lark Cove.

Maybe I should have bought a truck, like the one Logan drove in Montana.

"Are you comfortable, Wilson?" I asked.

"Yes, Ms. Kendrick."

"Would you tell me if you weren't?"

"Yes, Ms. Kendrick."

I smiled. "Liar."

His shoulders shook. A millimeter. But in our time together, I had yet to hear Wilson laugh.

I relaxed into my seat as my phone vibrated in my Chanel clutch. There were emails to return, and I had a handful of voicemails waiting. But I glanced out the window, taking in the city as we drove toward Midtown.

The city was a blur of steel and concrete and noise. Part of me longed to disconnect from the hustle, to retreat to the quiet lakeside town that my siblings called home. But who would I be without Kendrick Enterprises?

Who would I be without New York City?

This was home. What I needed was a vacation—or the semblance of one. I hadn't actually taken an entire day off work since, well . . . it had been a while.

But Thanksgiving was rapidly approaching. My parents and I would be flying to Lark Cove for the holiday, and it would give me a chance to slow down. For a few days, at least.

The blare of a siren filled the air and Glen glanced in the rearview mirror, easing to the side of the road. A police cruiser streaked by, weaving through traffic until it turned at the next block ahead.

Was Landon in that cruiser?

"Damn it," I grumbled with an eye roll.

That man, with his infuriatingly handsome face, had popped into my head more times in the past five days than was rational.

"Problem, Ms. Kendrick?" Wilson asked, attempting to twist in his seat.

"No." I shook my head, then dug my phone out of my handbag. The screen was lit up with notifications, but as I stared at them, I couldn't seem to get Landon's crystal-blue eyes out of my mind.

I blinked and opened an email. But halfway through my reply, I looked up, searching the street for that police car.

Not even work offered a solid distraction.

The curiosity was killing me.

Why had he come by the office? Why would he want to see me? He'd been dating Sofia, hadn't he?

I wasn't really sure what their relationship had been. Sofia had mentioned him a few times, mostly that they'd meet for coffee on Sunday mornings and to chat.

If she'd dumped him for Dakota, wouldn't Landon

want to be rid of the Kendrick women? Had he loved her? Had he slept with her?

I pulled up my sister's contact in my phone but couldn't bring myself to text. Maybe because I didn't really want the answers.

Why did I even care? Landon was basically a stranger.

"Glen, could you swing by a coffee shop?" I yawned. Too little sleep. That was the reason I was so hung up on Landon McClellan. My brain was foggy. Maybe this evening after my last meeting, I could go home early. Get to bed before midnight.

"I'd be happy to drop you at the office, Ms. Kendrick," Glen said. "Then pick up coffee for you."

"That would be lovely." *God bless you, Glen.* No wonder Sofia had loved him as her driver.

I typed out a quick email to Wynter, asking for the status of our kitchen remodel at Kendrick Enterprises. Normally, I'd get coffee from the chef at work. Except until the renovations were done, I'd be going without our chef's cappuccinos or lattes.

For years, we'd kept a small kitchen and a chef who prepared meals for business luncheons and employee functions. But I wanted to provide more options for our staff. So I'd decided to reconfigure the kitchen, expanding it to restaurant size, with industrial-grade appliances. Once the updates were complete, we'd be hiring a full staff and offering employees low-cost breakfast and lunch options. Plus, I'd have someone on staff to make me dinner for the nights when I was working late.

My chef and housekeeper at my penthouse hated the idea, mostly because I wasn't home often as it was.

Glen pulled into the private garage at Kendrick Enterprises, parking beside the elevator. Wilson was out of the car in a flash—for a man his size, his agility was always surprising. He opened my door, holding it for me as I slid out of the backseat. Behind his mirrored sunglasses, shades he often wore, even inside, I could tell he was sweeping the garage.

Besides my Cullinan, every space was empty. Dad had started working from home on Mondays, and since this garage was private for our vehicles only, it would remain empty today.

Regardless, Wilson was ever on the lookout.

His size was impossible to ignore, but Wilson didn't get in my way. That had been my only requirement when Dad had insisted on a security detail.

Without a word, I strode for the private elevator, Wilson following close behind. The moment we were inside and the doors were sliding closed, Glen was off to retrieve my coffee.

"I forgot to ask if you wanted coffee," I told Wilson as the elevator carried us up. "I apologize. Can I have Glen grab you something?"

"No, Ms. Kendrick. Thank you."

"Tea?"

"No, Ms. Kendrick."

Wilson didn't have a problem calling me Ms. Kendrick. So what the hell was with Landon? And goddamn it, why couldn't I stop thinking about him?

I stared at the stainless steel doors, my reflection blurry in the metal, wishing I could get him out of my head. The moment the doors slid open, I strode down the hallway toward my office.

"Good afternoon, Ms. Kendrick," Leah said from behind her desk.

I waved. "Good afternoon, Leah."

Wilson shoved his sunglasses on top of his black hair, then took up his regular spot in the lobby to keep watch. Every week he seemed to inch a bit closer to Leah's desk. The thought made me smile.

Leah was just over five feet tall. She was tiny compared to most, but especially when standing beside Wilson. She was never without a smile. Wilson was the epitome of serious. But every now and then, his dark eyes would crinkle at the sides in a barely there smile when he saw her.

We had a no-fraternization policy at Kendrick Enterprises. I'd hate to lose either of them, but maybe we could make an exception since Wilson was technically employed by me, not the company.

Someone should be in love, because it certainly wasn't going to be me.

"Wynter, five minutes," I said as I passed her desk.

"Of course." She scrambled to her feet, plucking a cluster of sticky notes before rushing to follow me into my office.

I dropped my handbag on my desk and plopped into my chair. "Okay, what do you have for me?"

"The kitchen remodel is behind." She winced as she stared at the top Post-it in her stack. "Sorry."

"How far?"

"The project manager estimated three—"

"Weeks?"

"Months."

I groaned.

"They're running into some labor constraints."

I sighed. Was I surprised? No. I'd already anticipated this would happen, so when they'd provided me with the original timeline, I'd mentally added a three-month buffer. Hopefully, it would be enough.

"What's next?" I asked.

"Your three o'clock meeting got bumped to five. And your four o'clock moved to seven. They're updated in your calendar."

Apparently it wouldn't be an early night after all. "Anything else?"

Wynter had three other sticky notes, each with updates I'd requested this morning. After she was done, she stood, just as Glen knocked on my door, a to-go coffee cup in hand.

"Thank you," I told him.

"You're welcome." He did a slight bow as he backed out of my office. "I'll see you this evening, Ms. Kendrick."

Glen didn't have any trouble calling me Ms. Kendrick either. "Yes, thanks again for the coffee."

"Of course." Both he and Wynter escaped my office, probably to confer over my updated schedule so he'd know when to be here to drive me home.

I sipped my vanilla latte, spinning my chair away from my monitor and toward the wide windows that overlooked the city.

The sky was gray today, the color of impending snow. Winter or summer, the seasons made little difference in my life. Rain or shine, my days were spent here, behind these windows with buildings sprawled in every direction, framed by bustling streets. The view from my corner office was the best around, though Dad argued his side of the top floor was better because you could see more of Central Park.

On the street below, a police car turned a corner, its blue and red lights flashing. Apparently, there was no escaping the NYPD today. Or thoughts of Landon.

Why? Why had he come here? And when I'd asked, why hadn't he told me?

Think I'll keep that to myself for a bit.

What the hell kind of answer was that?

There was one person who'd know. I turned away from the glass, plucking my phone from my desk to call Sofia.

"Hi, this is Sofia. I'm unavailable at the moment. Please leave a message. If this is in regard to the studio, please call Daniel Kim at—"

I hung up before she rattled off her operations manager's number. It was probably for the best I'd gotten her voicemail. Sofia had plenty happening in her own life, more important things than dealing with my rampant curiosity about Landon McClellan.

It just . . . it made no sense. I hated vague, and Landon had waltzed in here the other day and left me with enough ambiguity to paint the city skyline.

Mom always joked that I should have that tagline tattooed on my forehead—*State your purpose.* She was a woman who loved to talk for the sake of talking. I didn't have time for idle chatter and hadn't since the day I'd graduated college and taken my place with Kendrick Enterprises.

"Stop thinking about him." I sat in my chair, straightening my shoulders. Enough was enough. Effective immediately, I would stop thinking about a certain police officer and his soft lips.

I rubbed my temples, willing this headache to go away. It had been brewing since my lunch meeting. A meeting where I'd met with the CEO of a real estate firm. He represented a client who was looking to sell three buildings in Manhattan.

I had an entire team who managed our real estate transactions. They worked on the tenth, eleventh and twelfth floors. Above them on the thirteenth and fourteenth were the teams that managed our investments in various steel factories across the country. Floor fifteen was the team that oversaw our stake in two large shipping companies. And on the other floors, sprinkled between me on the fortieth floor and tech on the second, I had hundreds of other employees.

This real estate guy had insisted on discussing a buy-sell agreement with me personally. No matter how many times my senior vice president, Martin, had offered to take the meeting, he'd refused.

During lunch, the son of a bitch had hit on me three times. Pig.

I picked up my desk phone, calling Martin's extension.

"Ms. Kendrick. How was the lunch meeting?"

"Frustrating," I said. "I want you to contact the client directly. See if we can cut out this realtor entirely."

"I've tried," Martin said. "They're buddies. The client wants his friend to get a cut."

"Any idea when the listing contract expires?"

"One month, I believe."

"Good." I'd wait this pig out until the client wasn't on contract. The buildings had been listed for months without an offer. I'd risk it. "Let's test their friendship, shall we? Send me numbers on the highest possible price we can pay and still make this project pencil profitability. We'll see how tight these two are."

If the owner could make enough money, he might

be willing to throw his *buddy* under the bus, especially if it saved him a hefty realtor fee.

"I'll have it to you before the end of the day."

"Thanks, Martin."

He chuckled. "No, thank you. I can't stand that guy."

"That makes two of us." I ended the call and opened my desk drawer, searching for my Advil stash.

Except instead of a pill bottle, my fingers skimmed an invitation.

The card was decorated with a pearl satin–embossed border. The script was hand-drawn calligraphy. I lifted out the paper, running my finger along that smooth edge, then tracing Abel's name.

The accompanying RSVP card, still in the drawer, mocked me.

Not only had he broken my heart, but now, months later, the torment continued. If I declined the invitation to his wedding, he might think I had lingering feelings for him. I didn't, but he'd make that assumption.

Or he'd assume I was too busy. And that would just prove his point, wouldn't it? That I worked too much.

Abel had made me feel guilty for working. For my dedication. For being driven and competitive. Not ideal qualities in a woman these days, apparently. Though I guess it was better than a man who only wanted me for my looks. Or a man who only wanted me for my millions.

Was that why Landon had come to my office? The

money? If he'd failed with Sofia, why not try the other Kendrick sister, right?

The idea made my stomach churn. I tossed the invitation back into the drawer, then pushed it closed just as my phone rang. A frown turned my mouth down as I stared at the number on the screen.

I hadn't saved it into my contacts.

But I knew who was calling.

"Yes?"

"Hey." That deep, rich rumble sent a shiver down my spine. If Landon ever decided to give up his career in law enforcement, he could make a fine living narrating audiobooks. "How are you today?"

"Fine," I drawled, then waited.

"You at work?"

"Yes."

"Same. Just took a late lunch. Picked up a wrap at this deli a couple blocks from the precinct. Thai chicken with a peanut sauce. It was so good."

I blinked. Lunch? He was calling to tell me what he'd had for lunch? "Is there a purpose to this phone call, Officer McClellan? Or is this like your call five days ago?"

"Five days. Sounds like you've been counting."

Shit. There was no point in denying it. I could have said last week, but instead, I'd given a specific number. Because yes, I had been counting.

"I was just calling to say hi," he said. "See how you're doing."

"Seriously?"

He laughed again. "Bye, Aubrey."

I opened my mouth to correct him, but he was already gone. "Grr."

No. No more. As of this moment, I refused to give that man another moment of my time.

My vow lasted the rest of my workday.

Until I went home for dinner and opened my fridge to see what my chef had left me for dinner.

Thai chicken wrap. With peanut sauce.

"Damn it."

four

Landon

TODAY WAS A BAD DAY.

"Fuck." I read the text and quickly typed out my reply. *Should I come over?*

Not tonight. She's already asleep.

It was only seven. But I'd missed my window. *I'm off tomorrow. Be there in the morning. Thanks for being with her today.*

Of course.

I shoved my phone in my pocket, wishing there was more I could do. Knowing there wasn't.

This was the problem with being a cop. I loved my job, but my shift schedule varied, and some days, like today, I worked a later shift. It made seeing Lacy before she went to bed impossible.

Lacy's bad days were always hard. On her. On me. They seemed to come less and less these days. I wasn't sure if that was good or bad. But more often than not, I wasn't there to help her through it. Guilt was a motherfucker, and that bastard had been punishing me for years.

Should I take that private security job? It paid better. Money was tight at the moment—too tight. I'd have more control over my hours. But damn, I loved being a cop. The idea of turning in my badge made me sick.

"McClellan," Mikey called from the bank of lockers behind mine. "You ready?"

"Yeah." Five minutes ago, I'd been excited about heading to our favorite bar to watch tonight's game. Now, all I wanted was to go home. Maybe after some food and a beer, I'd be in a better mood. I'd stop worrying.

I folded the sleeve of my button-down shirt up my forearm, then grabbed my coat from my locker and tucked my wallet into my jeans pocket. Mikey rounded the corner, dressed similarly for the bar.

"You okay?" His eyes narrowed on my face. The man was a good cop for a reason. Too observant for my own good.

"Yeah," I lied, doing my best to shake off that text. This wasn't the first of Lacy's bad days. It wouldn't be the last, and tonight, she was in capable hands. "Who else is coming?"

"Rodgers, Baldwin and Smith are meeting us there."

"Seems like I haven't seen Baldwin in ages," I said. "It'll be good to catch up."

"Agreed." He zipped up his coat as I swung my

backpack over my shoulder and led the way out of the locker room.

Mikey and I were both officers at the Midtown North Precinct. Rodgers and Smith were both in the Twentieth, around Lincoln Square and the Upper West Side. But Baldwin worked in Chelsea, so we rarely crossed paths.

Baldwin and I had gone to the academy together. We'd been out for a beer one night, watching a game at Old Irish, when Mikey had walked in. He'd had Rodgers and Smith in tow. The five of us had been friends ever since and tried to meet up once a month.

"Man, I hope the Bills win," Mikey said as we weaved our way through the station toward the exit.

"They won't. And when you lose to my Giants, I just want you to know that I'll be there to rub it in."

Mikey chuckled. "Mark my words. One of these years, the Bills are making it to the Super Bowl."

I grinned. "But not this year."

"Probably not." He laughed.

The Buffalo Bills would be in good company because if the season progressed as it had so far, the Giants would be lucky to even make the playoffs, let alone the championship.

"Hell, that's cold," Mikey muttered as we walked outside.

I stuffed my hands in my pockets, wishing I had remembered gloves this morning.

The end of October and winter was upon us. I'd

been over by Central Park earlier and the trees had all been coated in ice crystals.

Mikey and I made short work of the five-block walk to the bar. The moment we were through the door, the scent of beer, mingled with fish and chips, made my stomach growl.

Better. Being with the guys tonight was better than going home and dwelling on reality alone. My mood lifted, but there was still room for improvement.

And I knew just the thing.

"Hey, I'm going to make a quick phone call." I clapped Mikey on the shoulder, then jerked up my chin to the other guys, who were already seated at a table.

"Want me to order you a beer?"

"Please." I waited until he'd walked away before I pulled my phone from my pocket. Then I stood close to the door, where it was quietest, and tapped Aubrey's name.

It had been three days since I'd called her for no reason.

Had she been counting the days again? Because I sure had. And I really fucking liked that she'd counted the first five.

"Yes, Officer McClellan?" she answered after the first ring.

I also really fucking liked that she called me Officer McClellan with that hint of irritation in her tone. "Just calling to say hello."

"Again with the hellos. Are you going to tell me about your lunch?"

"Dinner, actually. I'm out for a drink with some friends and to watch the Giants game."

"Then shouldn't you be giving them your attention?"

I couldn't help but smile. That sass was irresistible. "Nah. I'd much rather give it to you."

"Lucky me," she deadpanned.

"I'm at a little pub, not too far from your building, actually. Old Irish. Ever been?"

"No."

"Try it. They make the best fish and chips in Manhattan." Maybe if I talked enough about food and my favorite eating spots, she'd be inclined to share a meal with me. At least that was my plan. Talk to her enough that she couldn't forget me. And after a while, when it might not be so easy for her to tell me no, I'd ask her on a date.

"Sounds a bit loud for my taste," she said.

Every television in the bar was tuned into the game with the volume on max. Add to that the chatter and laughter floating through the room, and the noise was the best part of this bar.

It was raucous and carefree. To be heard, you had to shout, and the loudest person in the room was the owner-slash-bartender, Seamus. He lived upstairs in the apartment above the bar, and not once in years of coming here had I found another person stationed behind the bar. And not once had I walked through the door to see him without a smile.

"Now that you've said your hello and reported on your next meal, was there another point to this call?" Aubrey asked.

"Does there have to be a point?"

"Most phone calls have a purpose. And I'm a busy woman."

I chuckled, glancing at Seamus as he threw his head back and laughed at something one of his customers said. "Have you smiled today?"

"What?"

"Have you smiled today?"

The line went quiet.

That meant no.

"Then the purpose of this phone call is to make you smile."

"Why?"

"Why not?"

Aubrey huffed. "I'm smiling. Happy now?"

"Liar." I laughed, turning to the glass window that overlooked the street. "Are you at work?"

"Yes."

"Do me a favor, find a window and look outside."

She sighed, but even over the noise in the bar, I heard a chair rolling and footsteps. Likely some killer heels clicking. "Okay, I'm looking outside."

"What do you see?"

"The city," she said. "Lights. Traffic. Buildings. The clouds."

The view from her building had to be spectacular. That many floors in the sky, she'd probably be able to see for miles. Was she alone up there tonight, watching the world in solitude?

"I'm looking out the bar's window. There's a guy across the street talking on the phone and carrying an umbrella. Whatever is happening on the other end of that call doesn't look good because he keeps swinging that umbrella everywhere like it's a sword."

She hummed. Not a laugh, but I was just warming up.

"Want to hear a funny story?"

"Why do you even bother asking when we both know you're going to tell me regardless of my answer?"

"Glad you're starting to figure out how this works." She might not be smiling, but I was. "I had a guy come into the precinct today dressed as Batman. He had the whole getup. Cape. Face mask with the bat ears. Black body suit."

"Utility belt?" she quipped.

"Yep." I closed my eyes, picturing her face as I spoke. Hoping that the corners of her mouth were beginning to turn up. "He asked to see Commissioner Gordon. I told him that I was Gordon and we spent a solid thirty minutes talking about how to better improve the bat signal."

"You're joking."

"Of course I'm joking."

My day had been spent on patrol and getting attitude from two cab drivers who'd gotten into a fender bender. I'd been called a pig two times, and I'd had to haul a drunk bum out of a convenience store.

"Are you smiling?"

"Maybe. Barely. Anything else, Officer McClellan?"

Go on a date with me. The words were on the tip of my tongue but I held them back, knowing she'd say no. "Nope. You'd better get back to work. You're a busy woman. Bye, Aubrey."

"Bye, Landon." Her voice changed, just slightly, on my name. Maybe it was my imagination, but even over the noise in the bar, I would have sworn it relaxed.

Damn. I'd seen the woman twice, talked to her three times—more counting—and I was already hooked.

That little conversation had turned my night around. I walked over to the table, wearing an easy smile, and joined my friends. "Hey, guys."

"Who is she?" Baldwin asked, his dark eyes smirking as he lifted his pint glass to his lips.

There was no point in pretending he wasn't spot on, so I slid onto my stool and shook my head. "She's so far out of my league it's not even funny."

"Ah, don't sell yourself short," Rodgers said with his thick Boston accent. *Short* sounded more like *shot*.

"I'm not. Not really." I wasn't the type of man with

insecurities about my life. I had one weakness, and her name was Lacy McClellan.

"Gotta repeat my question." Baldwin leaned his arms on the table. "Who is she?"

"Remember that woman I was meeting on Sundays for coffee? Sofia?" I asked, waiting as four heads nodded around the table. "We went on a date not that long ago and both realized we were better off as friends. But her sister, Aubrey . . . there's something there. She's brilliant. Beautiful."

Mikey let out a whistle. "Brains and beauty. What's the problem?"

"Aubrey isn't exactly blowing me off." She hadn't hung up on me yet. "But she's not giving me much to work with either. She's a challenge."

"The best ones are." Smith grinned, tapping the silver wedding band that shone against his dark skin. He'd just gotten married three months ago, and I'd been one of the groomsmen.

"Well, I, for one, hope she puts you through the wringer." Baldwin chuckled, lifting his beer in a toast. "To our boy Landon. May this woman bust his chops every chance she gets so that he can learn what it's like for the rest of us to brave the dating world."

I laughed, shaking my head as I raised my glass.

"Hear, hear," Rodgers cheered, his bald head catching the glow from the nearest TV screen.

The bar erupted with noise as a chorus of cheers

filled the room. Our attention snapped to the game, where the Giants had just scored a touchdown.

Baldwin nudged my elbow with his, leaning close so not everyone would hear. "Does she know about Lacy?"

"No." Only a handful of people knew about Lacy, including the men sitting at this table.

"You gonna tell her?"

"If we get to that point."

I hoped we would. I was thirty-five years old, and when I looked into the future, it was lonely. I didn't want to be alone. I wanted to spend my life worshiping a woman. Memorizing her face. Making her laugh. Just like my dad had done for my mom.

Before their lives had fallen apart.

And I'd been left to clean up the broken pieces.

five

AUBREY

"MS. KENDRICK?"

I dropped my phone like it was on fire. It clattered, landing on my desk as I looked up to my office door. "Yes, Wynter?"

"I'm sorry. I thought you heard me knock. Am I interrupting?"

"No." I shoved my phone away.

"I just wanted to let you know that Mr. Kendrick is here." Wynter had standing orders to notify me when Dad was in the office. I didn't get to see him often enough, so whenever he was here, I always made it a point to say hello.

With every passing month, Dad's work hours became more and more sporadic. Mom loved that he was home with her more now than he'd ever been in their marriage. But I missed seeing him every day, walking the halls or in meetings.

"Thank you." I smiled as she slipped away, and the

moment the door was closed, I slumped in my chair. "Ugh."

My focus for the past week had been utter trash because every three seconds I checked my phone. For a missed call. For a text. Anything from Landon.

What was wrong with me? This had to stop. I rubbed my temples, willing thoughts of a certain police officer out of my head. *Gah!*

Landon hadn't called since last week, when he'd been at that raucous bar. Maybe he was waiting for me this time around. Well, he'd be disappointed. I didn't have time to call Landon, just like I didn't have time to obsess over him calling me.

There was work to be done, so I sat up straight, shaking my mouse to wake up my computer. Then I clicked on the latest email in my inbox, an update from Martin. I smiled as I scanned it.

The buildings we'd been trying to purchase through that sleazy realtor would be ours soon. After a few meetings with the client, he'd agreed to sell them to us directly once his contract with the realtor expired. So much for their friendship.

I typed out a quick reply and hit send just as a knock came at the door and my father strolled inside.

"Hi, Dad."

"Hello, darling."

I stood from my chair, meeting him in the center of the room for a hug. "Want some coffee or water?"

"No, thanks." He let me go, then walked to the twin white tweed couches in the office's corner.

I took the couch opposite his and cast my eyes to the glass.

Fat, heavy snowflakes drifted across the windows. It had started snowing about an hour ago and showed no signs of stopping.

"What are you up to today?" I asked.

He sighed. Not just any sigh, the sigh that usually preceded bad news.

"Uh-oh. What happened?"

"Got a call from William Abergel this morning."

I stiffened. William was one of our lawyers. He was a named partner of the firm where Logan used to work when he lived in the city. It was also the firm where Abel worked.

William wouldn't have told Dad about us dating, would he? That would mean Abel would have let it slip. But he was engaged. There was no point in talking about me, not anymore.

"Okay," I drawled. "Why?"

Because if there was a problem, William should have called me. Not tattled to my father. One of my biggest frustrations was when people went to him instead of me. It was a well-known fact that I was taking over Kendrick Enterprises. Dad had named me his successor, yet still, people—especially older men—still went directly to him.

"Don't get upset." Dad held up his hands. "He wasn't

trying to go behind your back. He called because he had a question on some changes I've made to my will."

"Is everything okay?"

Dad nodded. "It's fine. Your mother and I have been talking about our real estate holdings and how to divide them up."

"Ah." The Kendrick fortunes, those that were inherited, were managed through various trust funds. Logan was in charge of those trusts, making sure that every Kendrick relative was given their fair share of the fortune my family had accumulated through the decades.

For years, Dad had been the one to settle squabbles between cousins and aunts and uncles. He'd overseen both Kendrick Enterprises and the Kendrick Foundation, until we'd become adults. The foundation was Logan's. The business, mine.

It had worked perfectly because I had no desire to manage the family trusts or the foundation. And Logan had no aspiration to take over the business.

At least, I hoped it had worked perfectly.

Logan had forged a different path than expected. For generations, the oldest son had taken over the business. But he'd gone to law school and found a different passion. So instead of a son, Dad's protégé had been a daughter.

My biggest fear was that Dad considered me his second choice.

"While William and I were talking, he asked if I'd heard about 907 Mining."

I stifled a groan. "I'm on top of it. I know it's a mess, but the CEO has assured me they are turning it around. I think if we just give them a little more capital to work with—"

"No." Dad sliced a hand through the air. "Time to cut our losses. Walk away."

Walk away? We had millions of dollars invested in 907 Mining. I had taken a personal interest in that operation, and though in the scope of our portfolio the potential return was on the smaller end of the scale, it was one I wanted to see through to the end.

"That's not your call, Dad." I steeled my spine, willing my nerves to stop rattling. Reminding Dad that he was not the only person in charge never got easier.

"I know." He nodded. "It's your decision. But consider this as my advice. Walk away. William thinks the CEO is taking you for a ride by always asking for amendments to your contract. I don't know if that's the case or if the guy is just a bad miner. What I do know is that he's not mining enough gold to make it a lucrative venture."

"I'll admit the last season didn't go as well as planned." 907 had only produced a fifth of what they'd projected to mine. "But—"

"Aubrey."

Would he stop freaking interrupting me? "What?"

"Just . . . think it over. Objectively. I've been there. I've hung on too long when something was doomed from the start." His face softened. "It's not easy to admit failure."

Failure. Hearing that word was like being pushed out the window and plummeting forty floors to the street.

Was that why he'd come to the office this morning? To give me this lecture and call me on a bad decision? Had his own father done the same? Or had my grandfather left Dad to figure out his mistakes on his own? At the moment, I wasn't sure what was better. If Logan were the CEO instead of me, would Dad have made this visit?

There were times when I felt like everyone was holding their breath, waiting to see if I was capable of running this company.

Or maybe the only person holding their breath was me.

I didn't want to let anyone down, especially Dad. I didn't want to take my family's legacy and run it into the ground.

I didn't want to stand in line with my predecessors and be the Kendrick who'd stood short.

The pressure was nearly crippling.

I couldn't be a failure.

"Okay," I whispered past the lump in my throat. "I'll let go of 907."

Dad put his hands on his knees and stood. "Got any time this morning? I was hoping you'd take a quick trip with me."

No, I didn't have time, but I stood anyway. "Sure. Just give me ten."

"Come on down to my office when you're ready."

I forced a smile and waited for him to leave, then faced the windows again, watching for a few painful heartbeats as snow flittered from the sky.

Failure. That word hung heavy in the air. The sting didn't fade, but I unglued my feet and hurried to collect my phone, my purse and my coat. Then I stopped by Wynter's desk and had her shuffle my schedule so I could go with Dad to wherever it was he wanted to go.

He was waiting in his office, wearing a wool overcoat and smiling at his phone when I walked through the door. "Did you see this one?"

Dad held out the phone so I could see the photo on Instagram that Thea had posted of Charlie this morning. In the picture, my niece was wearing a puffy coat and a pair of snow pants. Her cheeks were rosy and her smile wide. She was squatting beside a snowman in Thea and Logan's yard, the creation adorned with a plaid scarf, rocks for its eyes and mouth and a carrot for its nose.

"I did see that one."

"She's growing up too fast." Dad sighed, this one full of longing. "She looks more like you every day."

"I'm glad we're all going there for Thanksgiving."

"Me too." He tucked his phone away, then extended an arm. "Shall we?"

"Where are we going?"

He grinned. "Shopping."

Shopping. Great. I didn't have time to shop. But I let him sweep me to the garage regardless, where his driver was waiting in Dad's Rolls-Royce Ghost—I'd inherited my love of cars from him.

Wilson, my ever-present shadow, squeezed into the front seat after opening the back door for Dad and me.

The streets were slow, traffic careful with the snow, and the noise muffled as we made our way through Midtown.

Just as we passed the police precinct, my hand reached for my phone but I stopped myself from digging it out of my pocket.

Was Landon working today? Was he in the station? Or on patrol? Why the hell did I care?

I frowned, tearing my eyes away.

"What's that look?" Dad asked, nudging his elbow to mine.

"Nothing," I muttered. Just a man who had infiltrated my mind like some sort of cat burglar. "Where are we going?"

"Chelsea," Dad answered.

Ten minutes later, the driver stopped in front of a shop with cluttered windows and a burgundy awning.

"Antiques?" I asked Dad. "Not your usual style."

He chuckled. "This is more your mother's style."

Yes, but Mom wouldn't be here rifling through clutter. She'd send her interior designer to do the digging.

Wilson opened my door, helping me to the sidewalk.

I lifted the pantlegs of my gray slacks, not wanting them to get wet in the snow. Then I followed Dad inside the shop, scrunching up my nose when we were greeted with a wall of must.

Gilded mirrors of all shapes and sizes were propped up against the exterior walls. The center of the shop was filled with ornate tables, each strewn with glass vases and brass fixtures. Apothecary tables. Hand-carved doors. Upholstered chairs, none of which had a pair. The aisles were narrow and only slivers of the faded carpet were visible amongst the clutter.

Dad didn't dally or browse. He walked straight to the counter and tapped a small bell on the glass case.

Footsteps approached from the rear of the building before a young man appeared from behind a bookshelf crammed with antique books in varying shades of brown and black. He wiped his hands on his corduroy pants as he made his way to the register. "Good morning. Can I help you?"

"Yes, my name is Thomas Kendrick. I called earlier about an antique ring."

"Ah." The clerk nodded, digging a set of keys from his pocket. Then he bent, unlocking the glass case and pulling out a tray of rings. He placed tray after tray on the counter, not like he was showing them to us, more like he needed to move them out of the way so he could get the ring Dad was after.

I slid beside Dad, inspecting the jewelry.

My eyes caught on a unique piece. The ring didn't have a jewel, but instead a stone, polished smooth. It was a milky white with green striations, like moss through a rock. The cut was coffin shaped.

"May I?" I pointed to the ring as the clerk continued shelling out trays and boxes.

"Of course."

I lifted the ring, placing it on the tip of my finger and turning it to inspect the gold filagree band. It wasn't exactly the style I normally chose for my jewelry, but I couldn't seem to put it back either.

"Here you are." The clerk handed Dad a rose-colored velvet ring box that opened with an audible pop.

The ring inside was an art-deco style with a large rectangular diamond surrounded by smaller gems, each cut in various shapes, some round, some square, some mirrors of the large rectangle but on a smaller scale. The silver surrounding the gems was notched with tiny lines, so if you dragged your fingernail over the surface, it would catch, almost like a zipper.

"I'm getting this for your mother for Christmas," Dad explained, tilting the box so I could have a closer look.

"It's beautiful." Though Dad's gifts to Mom were usually from a Harry Winston salon, not a dusty antique shop.

"I've been looking for a ring like this for years. Your great-grandmother had a ring like this. Lillian's got an old photo framed on her desk."

"I remember the photo. Not the ring." The picture had always caught my eye because even in black and white, my great-grandmother had been so like Mom. They were both gorgeous, with the same face shape, nose and mouth.

"The ring went to your great-aunt. And then to her daughter. But along the way, it was lost."

"Is this that ring?" I asked, shocked that he'd been able to track it down.

"Unfortunately no," he said. "I tried to find that one but it's lost. I debated having one made but part of what your mother loved about it was the age. So I've been searching for something similar for years."

My heart melted. Mom and Dad's love was something I'd always admired. It seemed as strong today as ever. As a kid, I recalled walking into the dining room and finding Mom sitting on Dad's lap, each with a coffee cup in hand, laughing at one of Dad's stupid jokes. He'd take her on a date once a week, no matter what else he had going on.

They were everlasting, like this ring, as beautiful today as it had been new.

"I think she'll love it."

"I hope so." Dad looked to the clerk. "How much?"

"Five thousand?" It sounded like a question. Maybe he was expecting us to haggle, but five thousand dollars was a bargain.

"Perfect." Dad reached for his pocket, then grumbled. "I forgot my wallet."

Because when you were Thomas Kendrick, you

didn't need it to drive, and his favorite restaurants had a tab under his name.

"I've got it." I opened my purse and retrieved my wallet, opening the flap. Then I pulled out a thick stack of hundred-dollar bills.

"I don't like you carrying that much cash." Dad frowned. "Especially after what happened with your sister."

"That's why I've got Wilson, remember?" I glanced to my bodyguard standing stoically beside a wrought-iron coat rack next to the door.

I preferred paying in cash, and just yesterday a courier had delivered ten thousand dollars to the office. I didn't have time for regular trips to a bank, and it was handy to have money on hand for situations like this one.

"Uh, do you need a receipt?" the clerk asked, wide-eyed as I handed him the money.

I pointed to the agate ring. "How much for this?"

"One thousand?" Another question.

I pulled more cash from my wallet and handed it over, then slid the ring onto my index finger. A perfect fit.

"Anything else?" I asked Dad, waving my hand around the space.

"No." He nodded good-bye to the clerk, then tucked the velvet box in his coat pocket, gesturing for me to lead the way outside and into the waiting car.

As the driver took us back to the office, I stared at the ring on my hand.

The gold was pretty against my skin. I'd always loved yellow gold. Maybe that was why I'd been so invested personally in 907 Mining.

The failure. It wasn't getting any easier to swallow.

"Do me a favor?" Dad asked as we eased into the parking garage. He dug into his pocket and took out the ring. "Will you keep this in the safe in your office?"

"You don't want to take it home?"

He scoffed. "And trust your mother not to find it? She's already been snooping for her gifts. She's gone through the safe three times. I've had to stash the bracelet I bought her in my golf bag."

I smiled and took the ring. "I'll keep it safe."

Dad bent over to kiss my cheek. "Think about what I said? About 907."

"I will," I murmured, then opened the door and followed Wilson into the elevator, letting it sweep us to the top floor.

That little excursion with Dad had cost me an hour, but for the ring on my finger—and the smile on Mom's face when she saw her own—it was worth staying late on a Friday. Besides, it wasn't like I had plans tonight.

When I got to my office, I locked the ring in my safe, then trudged to my desk, picking up the phone to make the call I didn't want to make.

A call to a mine owner in Alaska. A call that would put a crew of men out of work in the spring. A call that confirmed I'd failed.

"I'm sorry," I told the CEO of 907 Mining.

"I just need time. Another million, maybe two, to replace some equipment. Please."

"I'm sorry," I repeated, my steady voice betraying the turmoil raging in my gut. Without another word, because there wasn't anything else to say, I put the phone in the cradle and squeezed my eyes shut.

Damn.

My phone vibrated on my desk. I picked it up, expecting to see a Kendrick Enterprises employee name on the screen, but it was the name I'd been hoping for all week.

Landon.

Should I answer? The smart decision was to let it go. To move on. Yet my finger tapped the screen and I pressed the phone to my ear.

"Officer McClellan," I answered.

"You all right? You sound upset."

How did he know I was upset? Was I that transparent? "It's nothing. I just . . . I made a mistake."

"And you don't like mistakes, do you?"

"Does anyone?"

"I would like to say no, but I deal with a lot of idiots on a daily basis, and their behavior would argue otherwise." He chuckled. "What's going on? Tell me about it."

"In a nutshell? I'm taking over the company from my father and every decision I make is under a microscope. Because of my age. Because I'm a woman. Because Dad took Kendrick Enterprises to the next level and everyone is looking at me, wondering if I'll be able to do the same. I want to succeed and not just by maintaining the status quo."

Each generation of this company's leaders had doubled the fortune from the previous CEO. My father had nearly tripled my grandfather's success. I didn't want to be the person who simply kept the lights on.

"So what you're saying is that you have large loafers to fill and you're wearing heels."

A laugh bubbled free from my lips. A silly analogy but it summed up my feelings perfectly. "Exactly."

"Given how well you walk in those shoes, I have no doubt you will achieve whatever you set your mind to."

"Thanks." My heart fluttered at the surety in his deep voice. "Why did you call me today?"

"To hear you laugh."

Considering my mood when I'd answered the phone, a laugh was no small feat.

"Good-bye, Aubrey."

I really did like how he said my name. "Good-bye, Landon."

six

LANDON

TWO DAYS. AS MUCH AS I WANTED TO CALL Aubrey, to hear that sweet, quiet laugh, it had only been two days. I was forcing myself to wait three. My hope—foolish hope—was that she'd call me this time around.

The urge to break my own rule was so damn tempting that I stuffed my phone into my shorts pocket, pushed in my earbuds and strode out of the locker room that reeked of cologne.

No doubt it was expensive cologne, considering this was the nicest gym I'd ever set foot inside, but the stench was so overpowering that my eyes watered. The guy who'd been shaving at a sink when I'd walked in a few minutes ago had poured it on too thick.

What the fuck was I doing here? This gym wasn't me. I preferred the basement gym at the precinct, where there were no windows and the temperature this time of year was close to freezing. Where the only smells were stale sweat, metal and concrete.

There were no mats or fancy machines at the precinct. If you wanted to do cardio, you picked up a jump rope or pounded the heavy bag. If you wanted to lift, you used the free weights. There sure as hell weren't yoga classes or Pilates.

As I emerged from the locker room, each person I passed was in designer apparel. They didn't so much sweat as they did glisten.

Meanwhile, I was wearing a ratty Hanes tee that I'd cut the sleeves off of. No, this place wasn't for me. But at least my month here was free. I couldn't afford a membership at a pretentious Midtown gym.

And if I had to leave the force, I'd have to get used to more commercial gyms.

The florescent lights were bright this morning, combatting the darkness that streamed in through the wall of windows overlooking the street. The clock in line with a row of mounted TV screens showed 5:10.

My plan was to do a workout, utilizing my free month's membership because it had been a gift, then spend the day with Lacy. Tonight, I was lying low, cooking dinner and cleaning my apartment. Considering the size of my small studio apartment, cleaning would take about an hour.

One thing I'd say about this gym, it was relatively

close to home. I'd jogged over from East Forty-Sixth Street instead of wasting my time on the subway.

Another point in the gym's favor were their stair-climbers. They were machines with actual stairs, not pedals. I stepped onto one, put my phone on the display and was about to hit start when a swish of brown hair caught my eye two machines down from mine.

I did a double take. Then grinned.

Guess I didn't have to wait another day to talk to Aubrey.

What were the chances? I smiled wider, taking out my earbuds and laughing as I swapped machines for the one beside hers.

She had her own earbuds in, sweat beading at her temples as she climbed and climbed. When she noticed me at her side, she glanced over. Then she did her own double take, her jaw dropping as she nearly stumbled on a stair. Her hands flew to the rails as I reached over and hit the stop button.

"What are you doing here?" Her question was nearly shouted.

Aubrey realized it too late, cringing as she plucked out her earbuds and glanced around.

No one was paying us any attention. The twenty people sprinkled throughout the sea of machines were tuned into their own devices.

"What are you doing here?" she asked again, planting her hands on her hips.

My gaze raked down her body and fuck . . .

What was it about this woman? Just like the day I'd gone to Kendrick Enterprises, my body reacted instantly. My cock swelled. My heart beat faster and faster, like I had my finger pressed on the speed button of a treadmill. I dropped my gaze, willing my dick to stop twitching.

These gym shorts didn't leave much to the imagination and walking around with a raging hard-on was not the message I wanted to send Aubrey.

Three deep breaths and I had a loose grip on my body. Heaven help me if she bent over in those black leggings and strappy tank. But for now, I'd won the battle.

"Are you going to answer my question?" she panted, her face flushed. At least she wasn't afraid to break a sweat.

"Stair-climbing, sweetheart." I grinned when she rolled her eyes. "Normally I use the gym at the station, but I'm not on shift today and didn't want to go in on a Sunday. A guy I know owns this place. He hooked me up with a membership."

"Oh."

"Don't sound so disappointed," I teased.

"I'm not."

"Sure." There had definitely been some

disappointment in her tone. Maybe she'd hoped I'd come for her? "This is my first time here."

"Mine too," she said.

"I figured you'd have your own private gym."

"I do." She picked up her water bottle from the machine's cupholder, taking a drink. "My personal trainer comes to my place three times a week. She suggested I give this a try for a different atmosphere."

"Sometimes it's nice not to work out alone. Even if you're doing your own thing."

Aubrey studied me, her head tilting ever so slightly. "Yes. Exactly."

"You want to work out together?"

"I, um . . . I think I'll just do my own thing."

"All right. Probably better that way. I'm not much for slacking at the gym." I held back a smile when that fire sparked in her gaze. *Bullseye*.

Aubrey Kendrick wouldn't back down from a challenge. Neither would I.

"Fine," she clipped. "What's your plan?"

I put my earbuds in, then added twenty minutes to the stair-climber's clock. "Guess you'll find out. If you can keep up."

Twenty minutes later, I was regretting my decision.

Aubrey was in shape. Great shape.

Fuck. I hopped off the stair-climber with wobbly legs, then walked to a shelf and swiped up a hand towel, blotting the sweat that was trickling down my face.

Aubrey stopped her own machine and stood at my side, barely out of breath. The only evidence that she'd burned calories was the color in her cheeks and the damp baby hairs at her temples.

"Next?" she asked, arching her eyebrows.

"Weights." *Breathe.* I did my best to steady my lungs.

Aubrey had set her speed on the climber and I'd matched it. But it had been twice as fast as I'd planned on going.

"Lead the way, Officer." Aubrey smirked. "Unless you need a break?"

"No." I swiped the bottle of cleaner from the shelf, then went to work wiping down my machine while she did the same. "I'm lifting chest and triceps today."

"Okay." She shrugged, then walked to a machine to do tricep extensions.

Much like the cardio, she pushed hard with reps and weight, but still showed no signs of fatigue by the time we finished the rotation.

"Well, I don't know what you're paying your trainer but it's probably not enough," I said as I wiped my brow. "You win. I give."

She smiled.

My heart stopped.

That smile transformed her face, like the sunrise beyond the windows illuminating my city.

This woman was going to consume every waking thought, wasn't she? She'd just claimed sunrises. I wouldn't walk into a gym again without hoping to find her on a stair-climber.

My chest felt too tight, so I swallowed hard, nodding toward an empty section of mats in the corner. "I'd better stretch."

My hamstrings were already tight, so I took a seat and breathed through the burn as I reached for my shoes.

Aubrey joined me on the mats, bending to do the same stretch. Though I could barely touch my toes, she practically folded herself in half.

It gave me the perfect angle to study that tight, toned body. Damn, but she was sexy. Her ponytail swished over a shoulder and I fought the urge to take out the elastic and let it hang loose.

It had been an effort to keep my thoughts off her legs and how they'd look wrapped around my hips. While she wasn't looking, I made a quick adjustment to my dick.

"Tell me about this business of yours," I said as I stretched again.

Aubrey blew out a long breath. "What do you want to know?"

"Anything." *Everything*. Whatever I needed to

have a conversation with her that lasted longer than a two-minute phone call.

"At the turn of the century, my great-great-grandfather bought a bakery on Fifty-Seventh Street. It was the first of his business investments. It was the start of Kendrick Enterprises." Her voice was infused with pride. "He had a knack for taking a business and turning a profit. From the bakery, he bought a flower shop, then a handful of restaurants before he expanded into real estate developments. By the time he died, he'd built up a multimillion-dollar business."

"Impressive."

"His name was Logan. My older brother was named after him."

"And Aubrey? Where did that name come from?"

"My mother's grandmother."

"Family is important to you, isn't it?"

"Yes." No hesitation. A single word that spoke volumes about this woman's priorities.

It wasn't just a business, a job, to Aubrey. This business was her family.

I liked that. Because family was my everything. "Tell me more."

"You're very bossy." *Sass*.

"Not used to it, are you?" I smirked.

"I give the orders."

I winked. "Sure you do."

She leveled me with a flat look, but the hint of another smile was on her pretty mouth.

I chuckled. "Are you going to tell me more about the business or not?"

"It's investments mostly. We provide capital to large corporations. We're fairly diversified these days. But some of our largest holdings are in steel factories and shipping companies."

"Gotcha. And your building, is it all taken up by your employees?"

"It is now. We used to lease out the first five floors, but when my father expanded a few operations in the past decade, we needed the space for our teams."

"That's amazing." Forty floors of people working for Aubrey.

"Thank you." She ducked her chin, hiding a blush. It was shy, like she didn't get complimented enough and wasn't sure how to take it. "We have a growing venture capital portfolio too. Those are usually the most interesting companies."

"Tell me about your favorites."

Her dark eyes danced as she spoke about her passion projects.

That flower shop that her great-great-grandfather Logan Kendrick had bought was still part of their enterprise. It had become a national chain, but the original location was still in Gramercy Park.

She'd recently invested in a perfume company and

the first bottles would be hitting the shelves at Neiman Marcus and Bergdorf Goodman before Christmas.

Aubrey talked about two different tech startups and how they had the potential to change the social media landscape. She confided in me about a gold mining operation in Alaska that was about to go bankrupt.

"When you called me the other day, I'd just gotten off the phone with the mine's owner."

"Ah." I nodded. That's why she'd had such sadness in her voice. "Sorry."

She shrugged, then glanced over my shoulder for the clock on the wall. Her eyes widened. "Oh my God. Is that the time?"

I picked up my phone as she did the same, my jaw dropping. It was after seven.

I'd been here for over two hours, and it had felt like minutes.

Like the clocks had stopped.

"I'd better get going." She stood from the mat. "I've got to get to work."

On a Sunday, because I suspected that there was no such thing as days off for a woman like Aubrey. I liked that too. Her dedication. Her ambition.

I stood, watching as she bent to pick up her water bottle.

"Bye, Landon." Aubrey took a step, ready to leave, but then she turned, giving me that quizzical look again, her head tilted to the side. "You're not intimidated by me, are you?"

"Should I be?"

"Most men are."

I closed the distance between us, forcing her to tilt her head back to keep my gaze. "I'm not most men, babe."

Her mouth parted. Fuck, that was sexy. It was just the right amount for me to slide my tongue inside.

So before I could kiss her, I winked, then walked past her for the men's locker room.

Maybe this gym wasn't so bad.

seven

Aubrey

As Glen drove the car down Park Avenue, my phone vibrated on my lap with an incoming call from Wynter. "Yes," I answered.

"Ms. Kendrick. There's a police officer here to see you."

My heart tumbled. *Landon.* I glanced through the windshield to see exactly where we were. "We'll be there shortly. Can you please ask him to wait?"

"Of course."

"Thank you." I ended the call and dropped my chin to hide a smile.

Landon McClellan was a constant thread in my thoughts. In the five days since we'd bumped into each other at the gym, he hadn't called. He hadn't texted. But he'd been front of mind and enduring, like the butterflies in my belly.

I blamed that shirt he'd been wearing to the gym. It had just been a plain T-shirt but he'd cut off the sleeves to reveal those sculpted arms. The holes had been so wide I'd had a glimpse of the muscle definition around his ribs. He'd lifted the hem at one point, fanning himself and flashing me a glimpse of those mouthwatering abs. With his broad shoulders, long legs and narrow waist, he was an Adonis.

A pulse bloomed in my core and I squirmed in my seat.

Landon was pursuing me. So far, my futile attempts at pushing him away had failed spectacularly. But what if I let him win? What if I stopped pushing?

I had no idea what he wanted from me. Maybe revenge against my sister for dumping him. Maybe money. Maybe sex.

The latter, well . . . would casual sex with a hot cop be such a bad idea? Because Landon's body held the promise of a beautiful orgasm. It had been a while since I'd had a decent orgasm not induced by the vibrator in my nightstand.

It was Friday. If Landon was waiting for me at the office, we could go out to dinner. Enjoy a glass of wine. Head to my place. Have sex.

A series of checkboxes formed in my mind.

Not exactly romantic, but I was a busy woman. Romance was overrated. Been there, failed at that.

I glanced at the bouquet of pink roses on the seat at my side. I'd bought them myself today. I bought myself flowers nearly every week, though usually they were delivered from the florist.

But after talking to Landon at the gym about my family and the origins of Kendrick Enterprises, I'd been sentimental. Over lunch, I'd decided to swing by the flower shop and see it in person.

It had been over a year since I'd stopped in. The clerk at the front had no idea that my family's name was on the deed to the place where she worked but she'd been sweet and had sold me a dozen roses wrapped in coordinating tissue paper.

I needed to make more time to stop by places like the flower shop. It had energized me, much like talking to Landon about my favorite parts of the business.

He'd listened with rapt attention as I'd babbled last week.

Aubrey Kendrick didn't babble.

He was as unnerving as he was attractive. I'd never had the urge to lick a man's sweaty body, but as Landon and I had been talking, I'd had to fight the overwhelming desire to trace the long column of his throat with my tongue.

What a strange morning that had been. Wonderfully strange. The days following had been the same. Focus seemed fleeting at best, especially today.

The closer we got to Kendrick Enterprises, the harder my heart beat. That ache between my legs became a throb, and as we pulled into the garage, I didn't wait for

Wilson or Glen to open my door before I climbed out of the car and rushed for the elevator.

Wilson jogged to catch up, taking up his regular place at the rear wall while I hit the button for the top floor.

The elevator was running slow, it had to be, because the ride was excruciating. Until finally the doors chimed, sliding open, and I strode into the lobby, searching for Landon.

Except it wasn't Landon sitting on the cushioned bench seat across from Leah's desk.

"Oh. Um, hello." Who was this? Where was Landon? I shoved my disappointment aside and walked over, extending my hand as he stood. "Aubrey Kendrick."

"Ms. Kendrick." He returned my handshake with a nod. "Officer Bertello. I'd like to ask you a few questions."

His tone made the hairs on the back of my neck stand up. "Of course," I said. "Let's take this to my office."

With a nod for Wilson to follow, wanting a witness to this conversation, the three of us made our way past a wide-eyed Wynter and into my office.

"Can I get you anything to drink, Officer Bertello?" I asked.

"No, thank you, ma'am."

I motioned to the couches. "Please."

He sat on the edge of a cushion, taking out a notebook while I took the seat opposite his, sitting ramrod straight.

What the actual fuck was happening right now? If

someone was hurt, I would have gotten a call, right? If someone was in trouble, this cop wouldn't be asking me questions. Was there a problem with an employee? Those issues were typically fielded by Human Resources before they ever came to my attention.

Officer Bertello clicked his pen open, then held it toward his notebook, the tip hovering over the paper. "Ms. Kendrick, can you tell me where you were on Friday morning last week?"

Wait. What? He was asking about my whereabouts? "I was here. Working."

"And what time did you arrive that morning?"

"Six. I'm here every day by six."

Bertello made a note, then glanced up, his belly straining the buttons of his uniform shirt beneath his coat. "And did you leave the office?"

Last Friday? What the hell had I been doing last Friday? That was the 907 Mining day. "Yes. My father came to the office around ten. We went to an antique shop so he could purchase a ring for my mother. A Christmas gift."

"And did he buy it?"

"The ring? Yes." I held up a finger. "Actually, no."

The officer's eyes narrowed.

"I bought the ring. Dad forgot his wallet at home."

"You bought the ring."

"Yes." Why was there so much doubt in his tone? "I paid cash. Five thousand dollars."

"Five thousand dollars in cash?" Officer Bertello looked at me like I was absurd. He didn't have to say it because the accusation in his eyes was enough. This guy was calling me a liar.

So I lifted a hand and circled a finger in the air, reminding him of exactly where he was sitting. "Yes. Cash."

He scribbled something on his notepad. "And do you have the ring?"

"Yes. It's in my safe."

"Can I see it?"

"No. Not until you explain to me what this is about."

His mouth flattened into a thin line. "The owner of the shop is claiming that ring was stolen from her store last week."

"Pardon?" My jaw hit the floor. "We paid for that ring."

"Do you have a receipt?"

"No." *Fuck*. "I didn't get a receipt."

"For your cash purchase." He started writing again, and as the pen scratched on the paper, I glanced to Wilson, who wore a scowl.

"Both Wilson and my father were there as witnesses. The shop clerk took my money."

"Mr. Wilson, are you a paid employee of Ms. Kendrick?"

"Don't answer that." I held up my hand, stopping Wilson before he could speak. "Before we continue with any more questions, I'll be contacting my lawyer."

Bertello frowned.

"Have a nice day, Officer Bertello."

He clicked his pen shut, like he'd gotten everything he'd needed already. "I'll be in touch, Ms. Kendrick."

I stayed in my seat, glaring at his back as he walked out of my office. Then I closed my eyes, balling my hands into my fists.

Had he just accused me of stealing? Or had he been accusing Dad? I hadn't told him everything either. I hadn't talked about the other ring, the other thousand dollars. If he already knew about that, would he think it was all part of a lie? My stomach twisted.

"Ms. Kendrick . . ." Wilson trailed off.

I wasn't sure what the hell to say either, so I stood and stalked to my desk chair. "Please let me know if he returns."

Wilson nodded. "Yes, Ms. Kendrick."

He crossed the room, ready to excuse himself, except as he opened the door, he nearly collided with a police officer. The officer I'd hoped to see today.

"Sorry about that," Landon said, trying to sidestep out of Wilson's way.

But Wilson shifted, blocking Landon from coming any further into the office. "Can I help you?"

"It's okay, Wilson," I said.

Wilson looked Landon up and down before waving him inside.

"Hi." Landon gave me a wary glance as the door closed behind Wilson. "Bad time?"

"You could say that." I gritted my teeth. "One of your brethren was just here. I'm surprised you didn't see him in the lobby."

"He must have just stepped into the other elevator as I was coming up. What's going on?"

"I'm not exactly sure. But I think . . . I think I'm a suspect in a robbery."

"What?" Landon strode across the room, stopping on the other side of my desk and planting his hands on the surface, bending down. The expression on his face was so serious, so police officer, that for the first time in a long time, I was intimidated.

"Start at the beginning," he ordered. "Don't leave out any details."

I took a deep breath, then replayed the conversation with Officer Bertello.

Landon rubbed his jaw when I was finished, pacing in front of my desk.

"Why would I steal? It was five thousand dollars. I'm worth millions. This company is worth billions. It makes no sense." I flew out of my chair and stalked toward my bathroom suite.

The suite included the bathroom, a small kitchen and a closet. I didn't keep much here, but on occasion, I ran late, so I made sure to have a few outfits handy. At the back of the closet was my safe.

I punched in the code on the keypad, then ripped open the door, taking out the ring. Then with it in my fist, I marched back to the office, where Landon was waiting, his legs planted wide and his arms crossed over his chest.

"See?" I held out the velvet box. "I paid for this, Landon."

"Take a breath, Aubrey."

"I don't want to—"

"Take a breath, babe."

I clenched my jaw but dragged in an inhale through my nostrils. "How could anyone think I would steal?"

"Another breath," Landon ordered.

"I don't want to breathe," I snapped. "You know what? This is probably a scam. What if the owner of the antique shop is trying to score a payday? She knows we paid with cash to her clerk. He told her that I didn't get a receipt because I'm a fucking idiot. So maybe she made up this ridiculous story that we stole this ring, and when she threatens to take it to the papers, we'll pay so our names aren't dragged through the mud."

It made sense. It wasn't the first time someone in our family had been duped.

But it was my first time.

I wasn't a thief. I wasn't gullible. I'd just wanted to help my dad buy a gift for my mom. Scream. Cry. At the moment, I wanted to do both.

"Aubrey, take another breath, sweetheart."

I squeezed my eyes closed so I wouldn't cry, then breathed.

Landon moved closer, his large hands settling on my shoulders. But I kept my eyes closed, breathing in his scent. Laundry soap and a hint of spicy cologne, enough to be enticing but not overpowering.

I leaned in a bit closer, taking another inhale, before I opened my eyes. "I didn't steal this ring."

"I know."

"That guy, Bertello, didn't believe me. I could see it on his face."

"But he didn't arrest you. That's a good thing. Means he doesn't have enough proof to press charges. So, we'll wait and see what he finds."

I glanced up, his crystal-blue eyes waiting for me. "We? Doesn't this break some sort of cop loyalty code?"

He grinned. "I'm on your side here."

"What proof can I show? I don't have a receipt. I don't have a credit card statement to show I purchased it."

"Chances are the shop has security cameras."

"Yeah, but if she's trying to extort me, that footage is most likely gone."

"Have you called your lawyer?"

"No. Ugh." I grimaced, then stepped around Landon. "I have a team of lawyers but they mostly specialize in corporate law." Except for one who'd spent his early years with the defense attorney's office.

I walked to my chair, plopping down in the seat.

As much as I hated to make the call, I did it anyway, picking up my cell phone and calling a man I really didn't want to talk to, today of all days. While it rang, I glared at my desk drawer and the wedding invitation inside.

"Aubrey," he answered.

"Abel."

eight

LANDON

I DIDN'T CARE FOR LAWYERS. THEY TENDED TO MUDDY investigations and make things ten times more difficult than necessary. Except they were an inevitability, and I'd learned how to deal with them.

Aubrey's lawyer?

Definitely not a fan.

But I wanted her protected more than I wanted him gone, so I blanked my expression as he walked into her office.

He strode into the space without hesitation, like a man who was very comfortable here. And not because he was her attorney. His brown hair was styled, not a hair out of place. He carried a briefcase and wore freshly polished shoes.

"Hi." He shrugged off his overcoat, sparing me a brief glance as he draped it over the back of a couch. Then he walked to where Aubrey stood beside the edge of her desk.

"Thanks for coming," she said.

"Of course." He bent, like he was going to brush a chaste kiss on her cheek, but stopped himself. An old habit?

He turned, squared his shoulders and faced me. "Sorry for the delay, Officer. Now that I'm here, I'd like a few minutes to discuss what's happening with my client. If you'd like to wait in the hallway, we'll call you in when we're ready."

I chuckled, crossing my arms over my chest. While we'd waited for him to get here, I'd taken up a position by the windows, overlooking the city.

Aubrey had a hell of a view from her office. And not just the view beyond the glass.

She'd been quiet since making the call to this guy. She'd stayed in her chair but had turned it toward the glass too. Only when her assistant had informed us that the lawyer was on his way up had she stood.

Aubrey hadn't asked me to leave, and even if she had, I would have ignored her. This wasn't something you dealt with alone. Something my dad had taught me years ago: you didn't leave a woman who needed you.

"Landon isn't the officer who questioned me," Aubrey told the lawyer. "He's, um . . ."

"Landon McClellan." I strode forward, walking straight into her side and putting my left hand on the small of her back. Then I held out my right to shake his.

"Abel Zimmerman." He looked me up and down as he returned the shake.

I jerked my chin to the couches. "Let's sit down to talk this out."

The lawyer's eyes narrowed. And when Aubrey obeyed without a word, he stiffened.

Yeah, pal. She's mine.

Aubrey took a seat on one end of a couch, and instead of giving her space, I sank down on the center cushion, leaving barely an inch between us.

She shifted, crossing her legs, then cast me a glance. But she didn't shove me away or demand I move.

My intention was for us to appear as a couple. And apparently she was going to go along with it. Interesting.

There was personal history with this Abel. Enough that she was willing to put up pretenses, play along with an illusion—she'd realize soon enough I wasn't pretending.

"I don't know if you're the right person for this or not," Aubrey told him after he sat in the couch opposite ours. "But I figure you can refer me to someone if needed."

"You said you were questioned by a police officer?" Abel asked, shooting me a quick glare.

"An Officer Bertello," Aubrey said. "I told him I wouldn't be talking further until I had my attorney present."

"Start at the beginning, babe," I said.

She glanced at my profile, locking those pretty brown eyes with mine.

I winked.

Aubrey pulled in her lips, like she was hiding a smile, and gave me a slight headshake. Then the smile was gone and she sat taller, facing Abel.

I didn't like the strain that clouded her expression. Part of me wanted to put my arm around her, tuck her into my side, but we weren't . . .

Oh, fuck it.

I settled for a hand on her knee.

Her intake of breath was nearly inaudible. Nearly.

"Go ahead." I squeezed her knee, then nodded to the lawyer.

She took a long breath, and much like she'd done earlier with me, she gave him the rundown of her conversation with Bertello.

"Who was with you when you bought the rings?" Abel asked.

"Dad. Wilson."

"And Wilson is . . ."

"My bodyguard." She pointed toward the door. "He would have been in the lobby when you came off the elevator."

"Why do you have a bodyguard?" he asked.

"My father insisted after Sofia was mugged this summer."

"Oh. I hadn't heard." Abel frowned. "Is she all right?"

"She's fine." Aubrey waved it off. "What do I need to do for this to go away?"

"Unfortunately there isn't much to be done. We'll have to wait and see what happens next."

"Wait. That's it? What if he comes back here and arrests me?" She shot off the couch and walked to the windows.

"I doubt he's going to arrest you, Aubrey," Abel said. "You've got two witnesses who saw you pay for that ring."

"Three," I corrected. "The shop clerk. But obviously he's lying to the owner. Or this is a conspiracy they cooked up together."

"Yes." Aubrey nodded. "This has to be a scheme to get money out of me."

Abel sighed. "Most likely."

"It's fucking ridiculous." She spun from the glass, crossing her arms over her chest. "I don't have time for this."

"Right. You're busy. Working." Abel spoke that last word with so much disdain it had me shifting to the edge of my seat. "We haven't received your RSVP to the wedding. Did you get the invitation?"

Wedding? What wedding?

"I did." Aubrey dropped her gaze to the floor. "I, um—"

"We were waiting for my next shift schedule to come out," I said, standing from the couch. "Just to make sure we had that date free."

"Ah." Abel looked between the two of us. "So we can expect you both?"

"Yeah," I answered.

Aubrey stood motionless, staring at her toes. But she didn't object.

"Aubrey?" He spoke her name with so much familiarity it made my skin crawl.

She raised her chin, forcing a smile. "We'll be there."

"Wonderful." He stood and collected his coat, draping it over an arm. "Call me if something comes up?"

"Of course," she said. "Thank you for coming over."

"You're welcome." He glanced at me. "Pleasure to meet you."

Liar. "Likewise."

I tracked his every step as he walked to the door, then let himself out. The silence after the door closed settled like a heavy fog in the air. Until I dragged a hand through my hair and walked to stand beside Aubrey at the windows.

"When is this wedding?" I asked.

"The first Saturday in December. I appreciate what you did. Abel and I were—"

"Together."

She nodded. "He works for the firm that represents the company. It was complicated. We called it off earlier in the year."

Now he was getting married. And the bastard had sent her a fucking invitation, probably trapping her into going. If they worked together, she couldn't say no. If she said no, he might take it as her still having feelings for him.

Hell, maybe she did.

"You asked me at the gym if I was intimidated by you. Was he?"

"No." She shook her head. "But I think he was threatened."

Threatened by her success. *Dumbass.*

"I kept him a secret," she said. "It bothered him."

Well, I couldn't blame the guy. If Aubrey was on my arm, I'd want the whole damn world to know. But if she asked me to keep it quiet, I would respect that wish. I'd rather have her than nothing at all.

"I'll need a tux, won't I?" I didn't have a tux. Sure as fuck couldn't afford one, but I'd figure it out so she didn't have to go to her ex's wedding solo.

"I'll find a way to get us out of the wedding."

"Don't do it on my account." I nudged her elbow with mine. "I love weddings. Hope you can dance."

The corner of her mouth turned up. "You'd really go with me?"

"Do you want to go alone?"

"No."

"Then you won't have to."

Her shoulders fell. "About the ring."

"It will be okay."

"I could just go to the antique shop. Pay her whatever she wants. Forget this ever happened."

"Fuck no." I scowled. "Trust the process. Give us cops a little credit."

I didn't know Bertello but I'd be making a call as soon as I got back to the precinct. Baldwin would know him and he could tell me what kind of cop Bertello was. I'd find out if he was going to do his job the right way.

"I'd better get going." I sighed. The last place I wanted to go was back to work, but I'd called in a favor from Mikey to cover for me while I stayed here.

"Thank you."

I reached for her face, letting my thumb brush across her cheek. "See ya."

It took effort for me to walk away without kissing her. But step by step, I crossed the room for the door.

"Landon," she called.

I stopped and turned. "Yeah?"

"Why did you come here today?"

"You already know the answer to that question, Aubrey."

"Tell me anyway," she whispered.

I walked into her space and framed her face with my hands. "You're all I seem to think about."

"What about Sofia?" There was vulnerability in her voice, like she'd been waiting for weeks to ask that question.

"What about Sofia?"

"Do you have feelings for her? Is that what this is about? Are you trying to get revenge—"

I crushed my mouth to hers, swallowing the rest of whatever ludicrous question she was about to ask.

Aubrey froze and for a split second she was ice. But then that fire raged to life and she rose up on her toes, reaching for more. She melted as I swept my tongue against her lower lip and delved into her mouth.

Goddamn, she tasted sweet.

As my lips moved over hers, the world faded to nothing. The clock stopped.

There was no going back. Not anymore.

I held her to me, kissing her with everything I had. Her tongue tangled with mine, dueling as she clung to my arms. As I slanted my mouth for a deeper taste, leaving no corner of her mouth untouched, she moaned down my throat.

That sound shot straight to my cock. *Fuck*.

I broke away while I could. The pink flush of her cheeks matched the shade of her mouth.

I dragged my thumb across her wet bottom lip. "Did that answer your question?"

It should have been an easy yes. But there was still doubt in her eyes. So I let go of her face and took one of her hands, bringing it to my aching arousal, pressing her palm against the bulge beneath my pants.

"I don't have feelings for Sofia. She's a friend, nothing more. She never got this. She never got my mouth. What I'm feeling is all for you, understood?"

Aubrey gulped, and on a slight nod, she dragged her palm against my erection.

"Fuck," I hissed, closing my eyes.

It was becoming impossible to control my body with her around. I was seconds from carrying her to the couch and hiking up that skirt of hers to find out what she tasted like in other places, but the door opened behind us.

"Oh, shit." The assistant dropped a stack of sticky notes, each floating to the floor. She bent, scrambling to pick them up. "Sorry. I'm so sorry."

Aubrey stepped away, tucking a loose strand of hair behind an ear.

I gritted my teeth, adjusted my cock, then took a moment to think of Mikey's hairy chest.

"Sorry." The assistant was still struggling to pick up her notes.

"It's okay, Wynter," Aubrey said.

Wynter shook her head and stood, on the verge of tears—or hysterical laughter. Then she slipped out of the office, leaving Aubrey and me alone again.

"I'd better get back to work," she said.

"Same." I didn't trust myself to touch her again, so I turned and strode for the door.

"Landon?" She stopped me once more.

I kept my grip on the door's handle, letting it tether me in place. "Yeah, babe?"

"Will you call me?"

My eyes softened. "What do you think?"

She smiled. "Bye, Officer McClellan."

"Good-bye, Ms. Kendrick."

That smile widened, her eyes dancing. "Finally, he shows me some respect."

I chuckled.

And the sound of her sweet laugh followed me out the door.

nine

Aubrey

THEA AND LOGAN'S HOUSE WAS CHAOS. I CLOSED MY eyes, smiled and soaked it in.

Laughter and conversation drifted around the living room. Granny and Charlie were cuddled together on the couch, reading a book. Collin was playing Legos with Dad on the floor. Camila was giggling as Mom tickled her ribs while they watched a princess cartoon. Thea and Logan were visiting with Sofia and Dakota in the kitchen.

The noise wrapped around me like a warm blanket on this cold, November day.

I curled deeper into the chair where I'd been sitting for the past hour, replying to a few emails while listening to my family. This trip to Montana, a vacation, had been long overdue.

Not just to see my family, but to give me time to think.

Mostly about Landon and that kiss two weeks ago.

It had just been a kiss. Two weeks should have been plenty of time to make sense of it. Yet every time I replayed it, my stomach twisted in a knot.

Because it hadn't just been a kiss. It had been the best kiss of my life. Admitting that, even to myself, was terrifying.

The moment his lips had touched mine, I'd known I was in trouble.

Landon was the type of man who could consume my life. He'd already stolen a piece and it had only been a month.

What happened if I gave in? What happened when it eventually ended? What happened when he broke my heart? Wouldn't it be better to avoid it all from the start?

Sure, I was lonely at times, but wasn't lonely better than devastated?

My insides twisted. What to do? Walk away? Or let it play out?

Logan walked into the living room, surveying the space. "Who's hungry?"

"Me!" Both of Collin's hands flew into the air.

"What does everyone feel like?" Logan asked. "We can eat Thanksgiving leftovers for lunch. Or we could go to the bar and get some pizzas."

Besides this house, Thea's bar was my favorite place in Lark Cove. "I vote pizza."

"Me too." Sofia came into the living room, passing

Logan and plopping down in the chair at my side. "But I don't want to go outside, because it's freezing."

This week had been the coldest the area had seen in two decades. We'd all been avoiding the outdoors, staying inside where it was cozy. Luckily, Logan's house was massive, so there was always a quiet room or corner when someone needed a break from the crowd.

"I'll just go pick some up," Logan said. "Anyone want to come with me?"

I opened my mouth, about to volunteer, when Sofia shook her head and gave me a pleading look to stay.

"I'll go," Dad said, pushing to his feet.

"Can I come, Daddy?" Charlie asked.

"Sure, peanut." He smiled. "Go put on your coat and shoes."

She kissed Granny's cheek, then streaked out of the room.

"Any preferences?" Logan asked.

"Extra cheese," Sofia and I said in unison, then looked at each other and laughed.

"I feel like all I've done since we got here is eat," I told Sofia as Logan and Dad left the room.

"Same." She lowered her voice. "This morning, I told Dakota I needed to work out, so he took it upon himself to help me burn a few hundred calories. He did this thing where he pins—"

"Stop," I groaned. "Seriously? Do you have to rub it in?"

Sofia giggled. "Yes."

I laughed, about to change the subject, when my phone buzzed in my lap. I glanced at the screen, and for a split second, my heart soared.

"Are you going to answer him?" Sofia smirked.

"No." I declined the call and tucked my phone beneath a leg, reaching for a throw in the basket beside the chair, draping it over my lap. That was how I'd had to deal with Landon's calls for two weeks. I'd had to tuck my phone away, hide it from myself, so I wouldn't stare longingly at the screen.

So I wouldn't answer.

"How is Landon?"

"Persistent," I muttered, faking annoyance.

Landon had called a few times while Sofia had been nearby. Each time, I'd feigned irritation.

Part of me wanted to tell Sofia everything. To confide in my sister and tell her just how much I was beginning to crave his company. But the other part of me, the coward, had won out, and instead of a confession, I'd been avoiding this talk.

I'd managed to avoid it all week. But we were leaving tomorrow and now Sofia had me cornered.

"He's good looking, don't you think?" she asked.

Landon was the most beautiful man I'd ever seen. I'd thought the same the day we'd met at his police precinct.

"Yes," I admitted. There was no way I could effectively lie. The man was gorgeous.

"He's nice. Funny. Smart."

"Then you date him. Oh, wait, you already did."

"Is that what this is about?" She sat straighter. "Because we were nothing. We were friends. He never made a move and neither did I. It wasn't like that."

Exactly what he'd said too.

"Give him a chance," she said.

"No." I shook my head. "I've sworn off men. And I'm too busy."

"Landon's a good guy. Make an exception."

I stared into my sister's pretty face and gave her a bold-faced lie. "Sofia, I'm not interested in dating him."

"Oh." She blinked, like that had shocked her. Like she was disappointed.

I was disappointed too. In myself. *God, I suck.* But I didn't need the added pressure of my sister's expectations and hope. "He hasn't even asked me on a date."

"Really?"

"Really."

"Huh." She seemed confused, probably because Landon had asked *her* on dates.

All I'd gotten were a few visits and a string of phone calls. I wasn't going to admit to Sofia how much I longed for my phone to ring. Even when I didn't answer, I liked seeing his name in my call log.

And it had been there a lot.

Two weeks and I hadn't accepted a single call. But he hadn't given up.

Did he think about me as often as I thought about him? Had he thought about that kiss for hours?

A shiver rolled down my shoulders as I remembered the way his tongue had tangled with mine. The softness of his lips and the nip of his teeth. Never in my life had a man kissed me so . . . thoroughly.

Then the way he'd taken my hand and molded my palm to his arousal.

It had been the most erotic moment of my life. Not even sex had compared. He'd shown me exactly how much he'd wanted me, then walked out, leaving me wanting more.

Foreplay at its finest.

I craved more and that was part of the reason I'd avoided his calls. I was scared to hear his rugged voice in my ear, because I'd cave.

I was scared of exactly what Landon McClellan might do to my life.

"How is work going?" Sofia asked.

"It's good." I smiled, grateful for a change of subject. "Demanding, as always."

"You wouldn't have it any other way."

"I really do love my job."

Would Landon be just another man who asked me to quit? Another man who complained about my long hours? Right now, he was an illusion. Better than anyone in the past. Maybe that was the real reason I was scared to pick up the phone.

I'd had enough illusions shattered in my lifetime.

I wanted to keep his, for just a little while longer.

My phone buzzed again and temptation got the better of me, so I pulled it free. But it wasn't Landon calling, it was Wynter. "I'd better take this." I shifted, ready to excuse myself, but Sofia stood first.

"You stay. I'm going to find Dakota."

I waited until she was gone, then accepted the call.

Wynter had done her best not to disturb me this week, but business hadn't stopped just because I was in Montana.

She ran through a list of questions, no doubt attached to notes, then gave me the latest update on a lawsuit we were battling with a former employee. "Is there anything you need before your flight tomorrow?"

"No, we're all set." Dad's assistant was in charge of the travel plans for this trip. "Call me if anything comes up. I'll be in the office first thing Monday morning."

"Have a safe trip."

"Thanks." I ended the call just as Dad walked into the living room, his face flushed from the cold.

"The office?" he asked.

"Yes. Just getting the daily update."

"Anything from Bertello?"

"No." I sighed. "Nothing." Was that a good thing?

Officer Bertello had also paid Dad a visit regarding the ring. He'd had to trek all the way to Oyster Bay for that discussion.

Dad had let Bertello ask him one and only one question—*Can you tell me where you were on Friday morning last week?* Instead of answering, like I had, Dad had given Bertello his lawyer's phone number.

That's what I should have done too, but he'd surprised me.

Maybe Landon was right and nothing would come of it. Maybe after Bertello had learned that my story matched Dad's story, which matched Wilson's story, he'd realized we were telling the truth.

I was ignoring it until I returned to New York.

"Pizza's here," Dad said, clapping his hands. "Want me to bring you a piece?"

"No, I'll get it. You go ahead."

He smiled, then walked to the couch, holding out a hand for Mom. Then he tucked her arm in his and escorted his wife to the kitchen.

Out the window at my side, the snow-covered yard eased down to the frozen lake beyond the trees. The evergreens were dusted in white, icicles catching the sun as it streamed through the clear, blue sky.

Lark Cove was as charming as it was beautiful. In another life, maybe I would have settled here too, alongside my brother and sister. Found peace in the countryside.

My phone vibrated again, just one quick buzz to signal an incoming email.

As much as I'd love to wake up to this view each morning, Montana would only ever be an escape.

New York City wasn't just home, it was part of my heart.

"Aubrey? You coming?" Logan called from the kitchen.

I tore my eyes away from the view, tugged off the blanket, folding it for the basket, then joined my family in the kitchen.

After hours of visiting and playing with the kids, we enjoyed one last family dinner together before Mom, Dad, Granny and I retreated to our rooms to start packing for the trip home.

Our private jet would be picking us up around ten from the airport in Kalispell, thirty minutes away.

Dressed in a pair of flannel pants and an oversized sweatshirt, I stood at the window, staring out into the dark night, gazing up at so many stars they didn't seem real.

My phone buzzed on the nightstand. Story of my life. The most successful relationship I'd had was with that device.

I picked it up, my heart skipping at the name on the screen.

Maybe it was because I was going home, maybe it was because I missed him and he'd finally called when I was alone, but for the first time in two weeks, I answered. "Hi."

"Hi," Landon said.

Just one word. And I smiled. "I'm sorry I didn't answer when you called earlier."

He chuckled. "Which time?"

"All of them." I walked to the bed, pulling back the covers before slipping beneath the sheets and sinking into the pillow.

"How was Thanksgiving?"

"Good. I'm in Montana with my family."

"I heard. Stopped by your office earlier."

"Oh." Why hadn't Wynter told me?

"When are you coming back?"

"Tomorrow." I held my breath. Would he ask me to meet him for coffee or go out to dinner? But he just hummed.

Damn. Maybe he wanted to do it in person? "How was your Thanksgiving?"

"Not bad. I worked."

"Because of the parade?" I yawned.

"Yeah, partly. You tired?"

"I haven't been sleeping well. It's too . . . still." My penthouse apartment was far above the city traffic. The windows were soundproof, so it wasn't the lack of noise that had kept me from sleeping well in Montana. "I don't know if that makes sense, but there's a lack of energy. And it's so dark."

I didn't have curtains in my bedroom in New York. I liked having the lights drift in through the windows while I slept.

"Makes sense," he said.

"It's usually like this on my trips here. It takes me

the whole week to get used to it, and by the time I am, it's time to go home."

"Got an idea. Hold on a sec."

Rustling, then Landon put me on speaker. "You there?"

"Yes."

"Okay, listen."

I held my breath and closed my eyes, letting the sound from the background fill my ear.

Traffic. A siren in the distance.

I smiled, relaxing deeper into my pillow before I yawned again. "Thank you."

"Welcome." Landon didn't speak until I was nearly asleep. Then he murmured, "Goodnight, Aubrey."

"Goodnight, Landon."

Except I didn't hang up the phone.

Neither did he.

Not until long after I'd fallen asleep.

ten

Landon

Aubrey's floor at the Kendrick Enterprises building always smelled like lemon.

The scent was pleasant and subtle. Maybe every floor smelled this way, but as I stepped off the elevator, I breathed in the familiar citrus and grinned.

"Good evening, sir." The receptionist nodded, not bothering to ask why I was here, as I strode across the lobby.

Not far from her desk, Wilson stood post, his hands clasped in front of him. His face was like stone, no hint of an expression. It was the mask of authority, one I'd assumed myself many times.

I gave him a brief nod, then walked to where Aubrey's assistant was stationed behind her own desk, her fingers flying over her keyboard as she spoke into her headset.

"She has an opening Thursday at n-nine," Wynter stuttered, her eyes widening, when I didn't stop to check in, walking straight for Aubrey's office.

Aubrey was sitting behind her desk, framed by the dark night and twinkling city lights. Her brown eyes flew up from her screen as I walked through the door, narrowed in a glare until she realized it was me. Then they flared and the corner of her mouth turned up, just slightly, but enough. "Hi."

"Hey, babe." I walked around her desk, waiting until she swiveled in her chair to stare up at me. Then I bent and dropped a kiss to her cheek, drawing in her own scent.

Floral perfume with a hint of that lemon, like the building was a part of her. Or maybe she was part of the building.

"Why does it always smell like lemon here?" I asked.

"The floor polish." Her eyes raked over my plain clothes, the button-down shirt beneath my wool coat. Dark jeans that draped to my boots. Then her gaze locked on my faded black Yankees ballcap. A hint of color crept into her cheeks. "I, um, hi."

I chuckled, propping on the edge of her desk. "You said that already."

"I suppose I did." She tore her eyes away, glancing back to her screen and then to her phone and then back to my hat.

"God, I want to kiss you."

Her mouth parted. An invitation if I'd ever had one.

I bent, planting my hands on the armrests of her

leather executive chair. Holding those chocolate irises hostage, I leaned in so close our noses brushed.

Her breath caught. But instead of taking that pretty mouth and making a mess of her plum lipstick, I walked away, taking a seat on one of her white couches.

"Tease," she scolded.

"Consider it payback for you punishing me the past two weeks."

"I'm sorry I didn't answer your calls."

"Don't be." I waved it off. "You're busy. Holidays are hectic."

Yeah, I'd missed her voice, but I was counting on the fact that I'd hear it for years to come. She just had to get used to that idea first.

"Next time, shoot me a text and let me know you're all right," I said. "Just so I won't worry. Deal?"

Aubrey blinked, her head tilting to the side. "You worried?"

"I'm a cop, Aubrey." I saw the horrors of this world. So yeah, I'd worried.

"I didn't mean to make you worry."

"I know that. So just text, yeah?"

She nodded. "What are you doing here?"

I spread my arms across the back of the couch, relaxing deeper into the cushions. "We're going to this wedding on Saturday. Thought I'd better figure out the scoop so I can get a suit or tux or whatever. And maybe we can get our story straight."

"Story?"

"Of how you fell madly in love with me."

A laugh, so carefree and whimsical, accompanied the most beautiful smile I'd ever seen.

My goddamn heart nearly beat out of my chest. Christ, I was fucked. This woman had me on my knees and we barely knew each other. Which was the point of me coming here tonight. It was time to change that. Time to get to know one another.

"What are the chances you have time for dinner?" I asked.

"Like a date?"

"Yep."

"Chances are good." Her eyes sparkled. "I actually blocked out the rest of my day to try and get caught up from being gone, so I don't have any other meetings."

It was six, and when I'd come through the main lobby on the first floor, there'd been a stream of people leaving the building for the night. But not Aubrey. She probably stayed later than the rest.

"About the wedding," she said. "I'd like to take care of the tux for you. It's the least I can do."

"I can handle it."

"I know you can. But I'm asking to help. Please?"

I'd planned to stop at a rental shop but there was a plea in her eyes. "All right."

"Thank you."

"Have you heard from Bertello?"

She shook her head. "Nothing."

"I asked around. Called a buddy who works in Chelsea. Bertello is a good cop. I'm guessing at this point, no news is good news."

"I hope so." She sighed. "Give me five to finish up?"

"Take your time." I shifted, digging my phone from my pocket to scroll through the news while I waited.

A knock came at the door and Wynter poked her head inside. "I'm about to take off, Ms. Kendrick. Can I get you anything else before I leave?"

"Would you please make a note to have my father's tailor contact Landon about a tux? He'll need it before Saturday. And let Glen know we're on our way down."

"Of course." Wynter nodded, then slipped out of the room.

Aubrey stood from her chair, picking up her phone and bending to click her mouse a few more times.

I traced the line of her neck. Her hair was pinned into a knot today. There were a few errant strands by her ear and another trailed along the line of her neck. She was in a suit, a gray tweed blazer with coordinating slacks. Beneath she had a silk black camisole. On her feet were six-inch heels.

A woman of power who dressed the part. Fuck, but I wanted to peel those clothes away and worship her body. To kiss every inch of her skin until I smelled like lemon too.

I forced my eyes back to my phone as my cock

twitched. Tonight, it would be another cold shower and my fist. Apparently, I wasn't just teasing her, but myself too.

"Let me just grab my coat," she said, walking toward the corner and disappearing through the door that led to her bathroom.

I tucked my phone away, then stood and waited as she came out, wearing a thick black trench coat belted around her waist.

"Feel like walking?" I asked.

"My driver is in the garage."

"We could take a cab."

Her nose scrunched up, the reaction so automatic and adorable I threw my head back and laughed.

No cabs. Not for Aubrey Kendrick.

"Come on, beautiful." I walked over, snagging her hand and pulling her to the door.

We walked into the lobby, where Wilson was waiting outside Aubrey's office.

"Ms. Kendrick."

"We're going to dinner," she told him.

He nodded and turned, leading us to a hallway I hadn't been down before. Wilson stopped outside an elevator, holding a keycard to a sensor before pressing the button. It must be her private elevator.

The doors slid open and Wilson waved us inside.

Aubrey stepped in first, standing against the far wall.

I took the space beside her, and since her hand fit so perfectly in mine, I clasped it again.

She glanced up at my profile, studying me.

"What?" I asked.

"Nothing."

I squeezed her hand.

"Where are we going?"

"It's Monday."

"Okay," she drawled. "Is that supposed to mean something?"

"Monday Night Football."

"That doesn't answer my question."

"It will."

The elevator reached the garage and Wilson stepped out first, glancing both directions before escorting us to an expensive SUV. This rig wasn't the kind you found on a car lot. The black paint and tinted windows gleamed beneath the garage's lights. The tires looked freshly polished.

A familiar man hopped out of the driver's side to open the back door.

"Glen, right?" I recognized him from when he'd worked for Sofia. "Nice to see you again."

"Officer McClellan. You too. Ms. Kendrick." He gave Aubrey a slight bow. "Where to this evening?"

"Ask him." She wiggled her hand free of mine to slide into the backseat. "He said something about football, and I tuned him out."

I chuckled, shaking my head. "You know where Old Irish is?" I asked Glen.

"Yes, sir."

"Landon," I corrected. "Just Landon."

Glen nodded, waiting until I slid beside Aubrey before closing the door.

Wilson climbed into the front seat, and though part of me wanted to tell him he could be off duty tonight, that I'd make sure Aubrey was safe, I knew what it was like to be in his position.

He was being paid—and likely paid well—to act as her shadow. I'd let the man do his job.

We rode in silence as Glen drove us to Old Irish. Aubrey clasped her hands on her lap, but they were so tempting, I stole one, holding it on my thigh until we were parked outside the bar.

"Wilson, you don't need to come inside," Aubrey said. "I'm sure Officer McClellan will keep me out of harm's way."

Wilson climbed out of the SUV anyway and opened the door. *Good man.*

"You'd think I was in charge," Aubrey muttered, earning a quiet laugh from Glen behind the wheel.

"Call when you're ready, Ms. Kendrick," he said.

"Thank you."

I led the way, holding out a hand to help her to the curb. Then I tugged her behind me into the bar.

The noise was like walking into a wall and I tightened

my grip, shuffling past tables until I spotted an empty booth in the far corner.

I helped her out of her coat, then let her pick a side before taking the opposite.

"Monday Night Football?" She pointed to the televisions, all tuned into tonight's game. "I don't know anything about football."

"That'll change. Give me time."

She studied my face again, like she'd done in the elevator.

Before I could ask what she was looking for, our waitress appeared, setting down two glasses of ice water and menus.

The menus were pointless. The waitress hovered, impatiently chomping her gum. "What are we having?"

"Brooklyn Lager," I said. "Fish and chips."

Aubrey shrugged. "I'll have the same."

"Do me a favor?" I asked the waitress, pointing to Wilson, who was standing sentry by the door. "Make sure that guy in the suit gets dinner. Put it on my tab."

The waitress picked up the menus, tapped them on the table as her way of acknowledging my request, then disappeared into the crush.

Aubrey glanced around, sipping from her water. Her phone must have buzzed in her pocket because she took it out, reading the screen. Her eyebrows pulled together and she unlocked it, her fingers flying.

I watched her work, loving the way her mouth

moved as she typed, like she was silently speaking the words as they appeared on the screen.

The waitress brought over our beers and Aubrey was still typing, so I took a sip, more content to watch her than the game.

She looked polished and perfect. Probably the fanciest person to ever sit in this booth. Not a soul in the bar held her grace and poise. But while she'd objected to the cab, she hadn't once raised her chin or wrinkled her nose in the minutes we'd been here.

Aubrey reached for her beer, taking a sip before finishing whatever it was she was writing. Then she sighed and put her phone on the table, looking up to meet my gaze. "Sorry."

"Why are you apologizing?"

"For working when we're supposed to be on a date."

"Look." I leaned my elbows on the table. "I get that you don't have a job that ends when you leave the office. My job isn't always predictable either. I've got crazy hours and get last-minute calls. So how about we set a ground rule right now that you don't have to feel guilty for sending an email or making a call. I don't need apologies. Do what you need to do."

The waitress chose that moment to appear with two red plastic baskets lined with checkerboard tissue paper and steaming with fish and chips. She set them down and plucked two napkin-rolled sets of silverware from her apron. "Anything else?"

"Looks great. Thanks."

"Flag me if you want another round."

I nodded, reaching for the bottle of ketchup in the rack beside the table's napkin dispenser, ready to tuck in, but when I glanced at Aubrey, she was staring at me again, her eyes assessing and her head cocked to the side.

"What? You keep giving me that look."

She shook her head. "I guess . . . I guess I'm just trying to figure you out."

"Want some help?" If she needed to know who I was, I'd lay it out there for her.

"No." A beautiful smile stretched across those perfect lips. "I think I'd rather figure it out myself. I like it better this way."

I grinned. So did I.

eleven

AUBREY

I'D JUST EATEN A FRENCH FRY WHEN A GROUP OF MEN appeared beside our booth.

"McClellan." A black man with a wide smile clapped Landon on the shoulder. "Now I see why you didn't return my text."

Landon chuckled, reaching out to shake his hand. "You know a lot more about football than she does, Baldwin. But Aubrey's a hell of a lot better looking."

Baldwin extended a hand my direction. "Bo Baldwin."

"Aubrey Kendrick." I returned his shake, then did the same for the rest of the men as Landon rattled off their names.

"Rodgers. Smith. Mikey."

"Nice to meet you," I said.

"Appreciate you guys stopping by." Landon pointed toward the door. "Now go away."

"Tables are pretty full." Mikey glanced around the room, then to the space on either side of us in the booth.

"No." Landon shook his head. "Not happening. Besides, I think that group in the corner is about to leave."

"Afraid of what we'll say?" Baldwin teased.

"Yes." Landon chuckled. "She finally agreed to have dinner with me. I'm not letting you clowns fuck it up."

"Yeah, yeah." Mikey waved Landon off. "We'll get out of your hair. But we had to stop and give you shit for ditching us tonight. See you tomorrow."

Landon nodded. "See ya."

The four men all nodded to me before wandering through the crowd to find a table.

"Does Mikey work with you?" I asked Landon.

"He does. Baldwin and I were in the academy together. Rodgers and Smith are both on the force too. We try to meet up every month or so. Have a beer. Watch a game."

"You could have gone with them tonight."

He locked his eyes with mine. "I'd rather be with you."

I dropped my gaze to my basket, picking up another fry. It was the honesty that did it for me. Every time I expected Landon to do one thing or say another, he surprised me. He'd caught me off guard more than once tonight.

In the elevator when he'd held my hand, just for the sake of holding it. When I'd had to return an email about the wrongful termination lawsuit we were fighting. When he'd told me that he worried.

Landon's willingness to go to this wedding was as endearing as it was helpful. I had no doubt he'd look incredible in a tux. But damn, I really liked him in that Yankees hat too. He hadn't shaved today and his jaw was dusted with stubble. Combined with the hat, it gave him a casual, sexy edge that I hadn't expected to like so much.

Every man I'd dated in the past few years had been from the corporate world. Suits. Shiny shoes. Briefcases and Rolex watches.

One guy, Mitchell, who'd been a hedge fund manager, had held more regular spa appointments than my mother. He'd dumped me after a gala, admitting he didn't like that I stood beneath a brighter spotlight than his own.

Another ex, Steven, who'd worked as a swanky real estate agent for high-end residential properties, hadn't even owned a pair of jeans. Not one. He'd dated me for a month before ending it because I hadn't wanted to introduce him to my father yet. If it wasn't my dedication to work driving men away, it was my unwillingness to let them use me as a stepping stone for their own careers.

Landon was so . . . different. Stubborn, yet patient. Insistent, yet relaxed.

Wouldn't he want a woman who could give him more attention, a woman who was easygoing and light? Why me? What was it that Landon was after?

Those questions would only ruin our date. They'd wait until later.

"So you wanted to get our story straight for the wedding. What exactly is this story?" I asked.

"I don't know about you, but I'm a fan of the truth. We met through your sister after she got mugged. I went on a handful of dates with her. Realized there wasn't a spark and that we were better as friends. And one day, I decided to stop by her sister's office on a whim. You threw that sass my way, and it was like a timeout. The clock stopped. From that moment on, I was a goner."

Wow. That was his truth? My heart tumbled.

I'd had the same feeling that day he'd first come to Kendrick Enterprises, like someone had hit a pause button.

"That story work for you?" he asked.

I managed a nod.

"Good." He chuckled. "We don't know much about each other. Probably better change that."

I knew what he tasted like. I knew that his cologne was the most intoxicating scent on earth. But there would be work colleagues at this wedding. And I didn't want them asking questions that I didn't already know the answer to.

"Probably," I said. "What do you want to know?"

"Dill pickles or bread and butter?"

"Dill." I laughed. "Really? That's your question?"

"Seems important if I'm ever going to make you a ham sandwich." Landon grinned. "If you were stranded on a desert island and could only take three belongings, what would they be?"

"Hmm." I ate a piece of my fish, letting the breading and flavor melt in my mouth. "A brush, because I hate it when my hair is tangled. A sleeping bag, because I get cold at night. And a lighter, because I don't eat raw fish."

Landon's smile widened, his shoulders shaking with laughter as he chewed.

"Your turn. What would you take?"

"You."

"Me?"

He nodded, his eyes dancing. "You. You'll have the essentials. And I think we could have a pretty good time on an island together."

"I think so too." God, it was fun to flirt. When was the last time I'd just openly flirted with a man? Even Abel and I hadn't really flirted. There'd been a mutual attraction but we hadn't had . . . fun.

Landon was fun. My cheeks hurt from smiling.

"Why did you become a cop?" I asked.

"My dad was a cop. I grew up watching him get dressed in his uniform. Couldn't imagine wearing anything but blue to work. I went to a couple years of college, mostly because my mom wanted that for me. But it wasn't my path. Dropped out. Went to the academy. Never looked back."

"I like that," I said.

"What about you? Did you always know you'd be working for your family's company?"

"Yes. I was always fascinated by my dad's business. On the weekends when he had to work, I'd beg him to take me along. At night, I'd do my homework in his office at home, just to overhear him when he was on the phone. In school, when teachers would ask me about my heroes, Dad was at the top of that list."

"And you don't want to let him down." Landon's eyes gentled. "I'm sure he's proud of you, Aubrey."

"I hope so," I whispered. "I'm sure your father is proud of you too."

He gave me a sad smile. "I like to think so. He died. About two years ago."

I gasped. "I'm so sorry. I shouldn't have brought it up."

"Part of getting to know each other, babe. Don't be sorry. He passed a month after my mom. Breast cancer."

My hand came to my heart. "Landon."

"They were pretty wonderful people." He gave me another sad smile, then turned his attention to his food.

The mood in the booth shifted, cheerful to somber.

Dad had always told me to read the room. To gauge the tone, the tension, before opening my mouth.

Maybe it was foolish, but if we were getting to know each other, if the mood was already dampened, I wanted to get this next part over with.

"We've talked about my business, but we've never talked about the money."

Landon's face lifted, his eyes holding mine.

"It's been an issue. In the past," I said. "Before this goes any further, I think it's worth addressing."

"Think I'm a gold digger?"

"I, well . . . no." If I was being honest with myself, the answer was definitely no. He was nothing like those idiots I'd dated. Or the assholes who'd been with Sofia for her own fortune. So why was I even asking?

Damn it. Why had I brought this up? What the hell was wrong with me? Maybe the reason my relationships had always failed wasn't because of my work, but just *me*. Here we were, having a nice time, and then I'd brought up his parents before accusing him of wanting me only for my money.

"Landon, I—"

"Shit, Aubrey. I guess I thought I'd made myself clear."

This was the part of the date where I got dumped. Again. "I'm sor—"

"Yes." Before I could finish my apology, he cut me off. "I'm in it for the money. You're the only one who could afford to get us off that deserted island."

I blinked as a grin stretched across his mouth. "You're joking."

"Of course I'm joking." He laughed. "Look, I get what you're saying. And I get why you're saying it. I don't have a lot to offer. I'm a simple man. I live in a studio apartment in Midtown East that's half the size of your office. I like watching Monday Night Football with my buddies and would love to see the Giants win the Super Bowl in my lifetime. I take a lot of pride in my job but it's never going to make me a wealthy man. Not the way most define wealth. But I'm rich in contentment. That's good enough for me."

My heart. He kept squeezing it. "I think maybe you have more to offer than you realize."

He sighed. "This got heavy."

"Heavy isn't always bad."

"No, it's not." He winked.

I was falling for that wink.

"Tell me more about Montana," he said. "I've never been."

We spent the rest of our meal talking about Montana and the other places I'd traveled in recent years, mostly for work. Landon told me about his bucket list of places to visit, with Ireland at the top of the list and Lark Cove the newest addition.

My phone kept vibrating on the table. It was just something I'd gotten used to, but each time, I held my breath, waiting for him to shoot it a glare or ask me to put it away.

"Want another beer?" I asked him when our baskets were empty but for a few straggling fries.

"Nah. I've got work tomorrow. You ready to head

out?" When I nodded, he raised his hand, signaling the waitress for our check.

I reached for my purse, but he shook his head, digging out his wallet from his pocket to drop some cash on the table. "Thank you for dinner."

"Welcome." He shifted out of the booth first, putting on his coat. And when I stood to do the same, he held it while I shrugged it on and tied the belt at the waist.

His friends all raised their glasses as we passed through the bar for the door.

Landon jerked up his chin, waved goodnight and let Wilson hold the door for us to step out into the night.

"Glen is on his way," Wilson said, taking a step away to give us some privacy.

I cinched my coat tighter, trying to ward off the cold. "Want a ride?"

"I'll walk. It's not far."

"Okay. Saturday?"

"Saturday." He nodded, stepping in closer. His hands came to my face. One tucked a wisp of hair behind my ear. The other hooked under my chin, hauling me closer.

Finally. I rose up on my toes, my eyes drifting closed as I waited for his mouth.

But his lips never brushed mine. They skimmed across my cheekbone, leaving a trail of tingles until he whispered in my ear. "Goodnight, Aubrey."

Then he was gone, leaving me dizzy. He walked

down the sidewalk, his hands in his coat pockets, with that swagger and sexy hat.

Be real. Was this too good to be true? I watched him until he rounded a corner and Glen eased up to the curb.

Landon seemed too good to be true.

He probably was.

twelve

Landon

The doorman to Aubrey's building stood from his desk as I walked into the lobby. "Good evening, sir."

"Landon McClellan," I said. "I'm here for—"

"Ms. Kendrick." He nodded. "She's expecting you."

The man motioned toward the elevators, waving me past his desk.

My shoes clicked on the gleaming marble floor, and when I stood next to the elevator, the steel was so clear I could see my reflection nearly as well as I had in the mirror at home.

I adjusted my bowtie, making sure it was straight and in line with the black pearl buttons on my white shirt. I ran a hand down the lapels of my jacket and the overcoat that had been included with the tux bag a courier had dropped off at my apartment this morning.

This was the most expensive suit I'd ever worn. The coat too. The tailor Aubrey had sent my way had altered everything perfectly to fit my broad shoulders and biceps. The pants tapered neatly at my ankles. The shoes pinched, just slightly, but the cashmere socks eased the sting.

The elevator doors slid open and I stepped inside, hitting the button for the penthouse and keying in an access code, per my instructions from Aubrey's assistant.

Wynter had been very thorough in the email she'd sent me Monday with instructions, not only for the tailor, but also when and where I was to pick up Aubrey.

I wasn't sure what it was going to take for Aubrey to actually call me herself, but apparently it wasn't a wedding. Maybe the next time I came here it would be an invitation whispered from her own lips.

The building wasn't all that far from Kendrick Enterprises, no doubt because Aubrey wanted to be close to work. Its abundance of windows reflected the city's lights. It was a modern style, rather than some of the more historic buildings in the area. This tower oozed opulence and elegance, with a two-story ceiling in the lobby and pendant lights that looked like hanging stars. This was exactly what I'd expected for Aubrey. Tall. Sleek. Glossy.

The elevator's music was a smooth jazz, the saxophone crooning a lazy melody. A soft ding signaled as the car came to a stop and the doors slid open, not to a hallway, but directly to her sprawling penthouse. Perks of owning the entire floor.

Aubrey was standing in the entryway, her dark hair curled into cascading waves. Her makeup was artfully applied, her lips stained the same bold red as her dress.

The air rushed from my lungs. "Damn."

"Damn to you too." She smiled and walked closer, her hand coming to my coat. "Looking good, Officer McClellan."

"You're stunning, Ms. Kendrick."

The dress was fitted at her torso, molding to her breasts, and was held in place with two thin straps that contrasted beautifully with her flawless skin. The top was almost like lingerie, a corset with sheer lining in between the boned seams. Small, intricate red flowers adorned the material, so a dress that might have been scandalous was sophisticated and feminine.

The skirt had the same sheer overlay, also adorned with flowers, but a solid silk lining beneath that swished and swayed with her body as she moved.

Aubrey wore no jewelry except for chandelier diamond earrings that likely cost more than my annual salary.

She was grace and poise, wealth personified. And tonight, she was mine.

She gave me that sexy smile, her eyes sparkling, darker tonight thanks to the makeup. Then she took a coat off a hook, letting me hold it out for her to put her arms into the sleeves. "Shall we?"

"No. Not yet." I wanted just one more second with her alone before the spectacle of the wedding. So I dropped my lips to her ear, burying my nose in her hair to breathe in that sweet scent. And hint of lemon.

She leaned into my touch, taking her own long inhale, before leaning back to meet my gaze.

"Save that look for later," I said, loving the lust flaring in those eyes. "Or I'll ruin your makeup."

Aubrey laughed. "Promise?"

It took considerable effort to take a step away, to stop my cock from going rock hard. This woman was testing the limits of my self-control. "We'd better go."

"Glen is waiting to drive us. I gave Wilson the night off. He didn't say it, but when I told him I wouldn't be needing him to accompany us to the wedding, he gave me this warning look that I think was intended for you."

I chuckled and held out my arm. "Probably was."

Aubrey looped her arm with mine and together we walked to the elevator, stepping into the car. She pushed the button for the first floor and keyed in her code, then away we went, dropping from the stars to the ground level.

"Red's your color," I told her, studying her reflection in the elevator's doors.

"Thank you." Her gaze raked me from head to toe again, her cheeks flushing as she bit her bottom lip.

Fuck, but I wanted to take that lip between my own teeth. "You're not going to make this easy on me tonight, are you?"

"No." She laughed as the elevator stopped.

I led her into the December night where Glen waited outside beside her car, rear door open so we could take our seats.

"I'll apologize in advance for how much business will probably be discussed tonight," Aubrey said as we headed toward the Upper East Side. "I'm sure most of the lawyers from Abel's firm will be there. They'll want to talk. And there will likely be some colleagues too."

"No apology necessary." I reached across the seat, taking her hand in mine to lace our fingers together.

She apologized too often. And it was always about work. Why? Did she expect me to be annoyed by her devotion to her job? Probably. Probably because assholes from her past, like Abel, had made her feel guilty for working.

Well, eventually she'd realize that I wasn't a man who'd leave a woman for her success. I didn't give a damn if she made a hundred times more money that I did in a year. I didn't mind that she had long hours.

My confidence wasn't rooted in one-upping a brilliant woman.

My parents were likely to thank for that. Dad's

hours had been erratic at best. The same was true with my own. And never, not once, had I heard Mom complain. She'd supported him, effortlessly. And Dad had done the same for Mom.

She'd run her own housekeeping business, and Mom had found a lot of joy working. She'd grown her company, year after year, adding employees and services until she'd become our family's breadwinner. She'd been a star.

Maybe that was why Dad had crumbled after she'd died.

Mom had been his anchor. Without her, he'd been set adrift.

Aubrey probably didn't need an anchor. She wasn't impulsive or unpredictable. But maybe what she needed was a safe harbor. A man willing to be there when she walked in the door each night. A guy who would never try to deflate her sails.

Her hand fidgeted in mine as Glen slowed, easing into a line of cars. One by one, we inched forward as the drivers ahead dropped off their passengers. Until it was our turn.

I opened the door, keeping hold of Aubrey's hand to help her out, then gave her my arm again, escorting her inside The Pierre. We followed the line of people across the black and white checkered marble to the second floor, where we filtered into a ballroom bustling with conversation.

The hotel had beautiful views of Central Park during the day, but for an evening wedding in winter, they'd brought the views inside. The room was decked out with flowers in every direction, even arrangements that hung from the ceiling. Candles added ambience to the chandeliers, casting the room in a warm glow. Other than an open dance floor, the space was filled with tables covered in white linens and bouquets of white and green.

Waiters with trays of champagne served men dressed in similar black tuxedos and women in every shade of ballgown. The ceremony had taken place earlier in the day, apparently at the bride's church, so tonight would only be the reception. But they'd invited what seemed like every member of the city's elite.

"Aubrey." We'd just checked our coats and barely stepped into the ballroom when an older man walked over.

"Hi, William." She leaned in so he could press his cheek to hers. "Let me introduce you to Landon McClellan. Landon, this is William Abergel."

"Pleasure," I said, extending my hand.

He dismissed me almost immediately, stepping closer to Aubrey and lowering his voice. "I need some time on Monday to discuss a few issues."

"Okay." She nodded. "Anything urgent?"

"No. But I meant to call you yesterday and the day got away from me. You know how it goes."

She nodded. "I do."

"I believe we're seated at the same table. I'll let you get some champagne. We'll catch up later."

"Okay." She smiled but it didn't reach her eyes.

"Nice to meet you," William told me, then slipped past us to talk to someone else.

"He's one of our lawyers," she told me.

"The enemy," I teased, flagging down a waiter for two flutes of champagne.

Aubrey had barely taken a sip when the next person rushed to her side.

One after the next, people clamored to her side, contending for her attention. I did my best to remember their names, simply because these people were part of Aubrey's world.

So was I.

Or . . . I wanted to be.

"That's where we're seated." Aubrey pointed to a table where William was already sitting beside a woman with graying blond hair.

The rest of the chairs were occupied too, some faces familiar, and every expression far too serious for a wedding reception.

I took Aubrey's hand, leading her over, then held out her chair so she could take a seat. Maybe I was a fool for not being nervous, but as I took my own chair, I relaxed into the cushion, taking in the beautiful woman at my side.

It was as clear as the crystal water goblets that I was out of place. Not just here at The Pierre, but at her building. Like I'd told the guys, she was out of my damn league.

But someone would have to tear me out of this chair to make me leave her side.

Eventually, I'd get used to this crowd, right? Hell, even if I didn't, who cared? As long as I had Aubrey, I'd deal with the pretentious snubs.

As Aubrey had expected, the conversation at our table quickly turned to business. She did her best to steer it away from work, but everyone else was relentless. Even as Abel and his new bride came into the room, earning a standing round of applause as they went to the head table, the conversation immediately returned to work once we'd resumed our seats.

"Sorry." Aubrey sighed as the first course was served.

"What did I tell you about the apologies?" I leaned over and brushed a kiss to her cheek. Then I ate my dinner, watching as Aubrey grew more and more annoyed when each of the men at the table kept bringing up investment opportunities or new real estate developments or *Did you hear about so and so?*

Finally, she earned a reprieve when the toasts began, followed by the newlyweds' first dance. When the lead singer of the live band welcomed other couples to the floor, I didn't waste my opportunity to get her the hell out of that chair.

"If you'll excuse us." I stood, pulling out Aubrey's chair. "I'm going to dance with my gorgeous date."

She took my hand and let me lead her to the floor and sweep her into my arms. "Bored yet?"

I chuckled. "With you? Never."

"I'm—"

"No apologies, Aubrey." I held her closer, until there wasn't an inch of space between us.

It was dangerous. No doubt she could feel how much I wanted her. But from over her head, I spotted Abel.

His eyes were aimed at the dance floor. His eyes were on Aubrey. *Prick.*

Maybe he regretted letting her go, even on his fucking wedding day. I had no idea who his bride was, but when it came to the women in this room, not a soul had Aubrey's beauty.

I leaned in closer, kissing her temple, then turned my back on Abel, shielding her from his view.

"Thank you for coming with me," she said, a smile lighting her face.

No doubt whenever I drove past The Pierre again, I'd see her like this.

Red dress. Pretty eyes. A smile, just for me.

"Welcome, babe."

"You're a great fake boyfriend."

I stopped dancing, waiting until her face turned up. Waiting until she had her eyes glued to mine. "This has never been fake, sweetheart."

She bit that lower lip again. "How do you feel about wedding cake?"

"Depends on how you feel about wedding cake. If you like it enough to stick around and have a piece, then I like cake. If you're thinking we duck out of here and skip it, then I don't really like cake."

Her smile widened. "I hate wedding cake."

thirteen

Aubrey

By the time we pulled up to the front of my building, my entire body was trembling with desire. Weeks of foreplay culminating in that dance. I wanted Landon more than I needed my next breath.

He opened the SUV's door before we'd even come to a complete stop, then his hand clasped mine as he dragged me across the sidewalk for the lobby's doors.

I smiled, loving that he was in as much of a hurry to get upstairs as I was.

"Good evening, Ms. Kendrick." The doorman was new to the building as of this week, and I'd been meaning to get his name. It would have to wait until later.

Landon didn't slow his stride across the foyer, straight for the elevator. He punched the button, and when the doors slid open, he moved so fast I nearly got whiplash.

His hand let go of mine so he could swing me into his arms, hauling me off my feet and against his strong body as he carried me inside. He held me tight, punching in the code for my floor, then the moment the doors began to close, his mouth crushed mine.

I moaned, opening for him instantly. His tongue swept across my lower lip before tangling with mine as he licked and sucked. His urgency matched my own. We kissed with a frenzy, barely breathing as I clung to those broad shoulders.

The elevator opened. A ding sounded somewhere above my head. But I was so lost in Landon that I barely recognized where we were going. All I felt was his heartbeat crashing against my own. We were moving. His shoes clicked on my floor.

Then he tore his mouth away and I whimpered, forcing my eyes open.

The penthouse. We were already in the penthouse.

"Bedroom?"

"To the left," I panted.

He shifted, taking us down a hallway. All while my feet hovered above the floor, like they were floating. His hold on me never faltered as I gave him directions, weaving through the halls of my home until he walked through the double doors of my suite.

The room was dark, the large windows letting in enough light to cast the space in gray shadows and muted tones. Beyond the glass, snow was falling, the flakes catching the city lights. Thank God for that light. Tonight, I wanted to see Landon's face. I wanted to notice every shadow, every expression, as he came apart.

He set me on my feet and took a step away, his eyes narrowing as he looked at me. Three seconds passed. Four. My heart pounded as he stood there and watched.

"What?" Why wasn't he moving? I needed him to touch me. To kiss me. To fuck me senseless.

"You."

"What about me?" My voice was nearly shaking.

"You'll own me after this."

My breath hitched. That honesty, that raw truth. He never said what I expected. "Does that worry you?"

"Not a damn bit." He crooked a finger, beckoning me closer.

I moved on unsteady legs, my knees weak, until I was standing before him, my neck craned to hold his gaze.

His large hands came to my face, pushing the hair away from my temples. "Aubrey."

Landon spoke my name the way I'd wished upon the stars as a little girl.

In unison, we shrugged off our coats. My fingers went to the buttons on his jacket, setting them free.

His eyes flared, those pools darkening. "Keep going."

I bit my lower lip to hide a smile as my hands roved up the plane of his chest, moving to his shoulders to push away the jacket. Then I tugged at his bowtie, loosening it from his neck.

"Take my shirt off." His gravelly voice sent a shiver down my spine.

I obeyed, working the buttons free until I pulled the crisp shirt from the hem of his slacks. And just like I'd done with the jacket, I moved up his chest, this time my palms dragging against his hot skin, until I shoved the shirt to the floor, his clothes pooling by our feet.

"Kick off your shoes," I said, wanting to drop to my knees and pull those pants from his legs.

Landon shook his head, taking my chin in his hand. He waited until I began to squirm. Fuck, it was hot being at his mercy.

"Landon," I pleaded.

"I give the orders, yes?"

I gulped. "Yes."

The corner of his mouth turned up in a wicked grin as he toed off his shoes.

I wanted to taste him, but when I made a move to drop to my knees, he tightened his grip on my chin and shook his head. I straightened. And waited for his next command.

Approval gleamed in his eyes. "Turn around."

I obeyed. Who was I? Not a woman who took orders well. Not a woman who liked giving up control. But it came so naturally, this surrender, that my head began to spin. My breath came in short pants, my nerve endings abuzz.

Landon trailed his fingertips across my shoulder.

One move and my pussy clenched. Never in my life had I been this turned on. This desperate for a release. And he'd barely touched me.

Was that the point of those calls? Those brief encounters in my office? The first kiss? All this time, had he been working toward this moment? The tension had me strung tight, like a rubber band about to snap.

Landon's lips replaced his fingers, his tongue leaving a wet trail on my skin as his hands went to the zipper on the dress, releasing it inch by painstaking inch. He slid the straps free, letting it fall past my waist.

My nipples hardened, the cool air rushing to my overheated skin.

Landon's hands came to my hair, threading through the waves. He began to pull the strands, gently, but with enough pressure to tilt my head backward. One hand held the locks while the other came to my scalp, then dragged the mass through his fist, one hand replacing the other over and over again, like he was creating a ponytail.

Then he held it, wrapping it around a fist while his other hand skated across my ribs to my belly, trailing up my sternum and shifting to cup a breast.

I arched into him, pinned at my hair and unable to turn. Did I like this? *Yes.* It was freeing, letting go.

His fingers rolled a nipple, giving it a slight pinch that shot a wave of desire to my core. His mouth latched on to my neck, sucking and licking until every vein and artery in my body pulsed.

If this was foreplay, I'd let him play with me for eternity.

"Landon."

He slid his hand to the other breast, giving that nipple a hard pinch.

"Oh, God," I hissed.

"Like that?" His deep chuckle filled my ear as his hand trailed down my belly, cupping my mound.

I gasped, my legs already trembling, as his fingers slipped beneath my panties to run through my folds.

"You're drenched."

"Yes." I rocked against his hand, needing just a bit more friction.

"How expensive are these panties?" he asked, but he didn't wait for my answer before he shifted to my hip, grabbing the lace and tearing it from my body. He tore that lace like it was tissue paper.

I whimpered.

Landon inched closer, his erection pressing against my ass.

I reached behind me, feeling for it. If he'd been hard the day in my office after our kiss, tonight, he was steel. I palmed his length, letting him press it into my hand. God, I wanted to touch him. To take his shaft in my hand, my mouth, and watch him come undone. But his grip on my hair tightened, a silent reminder that I was not in control.

It was unnerving. Frustrating. Thrilling. Erotic.

"This is driving you wild, isn't it, babe?" Landon's lips caressed the shell of my ear as he spoke.

"Yes," I admitted.

"You'll learn to love it." His fingers slipped through my slit once more, coating himself in my wetness before he grazed my clit.

I gasped as a ripple rolled through my body.

"Turn around," he ordered, letting go of my hair, and as I spun, his arms banded around me, his mouth sealing over mine. His hands roamed up and down my bare skin, touching every inch, molding every curve. His tongue drew lazy circles against my own.

It was a different sort of urgency. Not frantic or hurried. We kissed like we were desperate to memorize each other's secrets.

Landon kept his lips on mine as he rifled through his pocket before unzipping his slacks and shoving them to the floor. His erection bobbed free, hard and thick between us, as he picked me up again and carried me to the bed.

I sank into the mattress as his weight came down on mine, settling into the cradle of my hips.

His hands came to mine, stretching and lifting them above my head. "Don't move them."

Fisting a pillow, I watched as he hovered over me, dropping kisses along my collarbones until he lowered to take a nipple in his mouth.

I closed my eyes, melting as his tongue swirled. Did

he know how much I loved this? How sensitive my nipples were and how much I loved his hot mouth?

Landon moved to the other breast, giving that nipple the same treatment, until I writhed beneath him, desperate for more.

My legs widened. My core ached. The sound of a tearing condom wrapper filled the room.

His tongue moved across my skin, back to my neck, until he found my lips again. Then one hand came to mine, holding my wrists together, as his other guided his cock, positioning it at my entrance.

"Fuck, but you are gorgeous." He kissed the corner of my mouth. "Look at me."

I opened, meeting his gaze, as he rocked us together, slowly, until he was buried inside me. "Oh, fuck."

Oh, he was big. It took my body a moment to stretch around him and relax. Then a wave of pleasure hit, like I was melting.

"You're so tight." He let go of my wrists. "I'm going to fuck you hard, babe."

"Yes," I moaned.

"Hold on."

My hands went to his shoulders but he didn't like where I'd placed them, so he repositioned them, exactly where he wanted. Then he eased out, only to thrust in. Hard, as promised. My body quaked, my limbs beginning to tremble.

"One of these times, I'm going to put you in my handcuffs," he murmured.

My pussy clenched.

"You like that idea, don't you?" He didn't let me answer. He pulled out and slammed inside, stealing any words.

He brought us together, over and over, the sound of our bodies and ragged breaths filling the room. A string of incoherent moans escaped my lips. White stars creeped in at the edges of my vision until I squeezed my eyes shut.

"Not yet." Landon gritted his teeth as my inner walls fluttered. "Do not come."

"I need—"

"Not. Yet."

My eyes popped open, shooting him a glare. It only earned me a sexy smirk as he kept fucking me. His jaw clenched as he moved. His face like granite as he chased his own release.

It was impossible, trying to hold back when every cell in my body felt like it was coming apart. My nails dug into his skin, my teeth sunk into my bottom lip.

Until finally, he pinched a nipple and whispered, "Come."

I shattered.

I broke into a million tiny pieces as I cried his name. My body trembled, shudder after shudder of the longest, most incredible orgasm of my life. My core pulsed, clenching around him as he pistoned faster.

"Aubrey," he murmured. "Fucking hell." Then he buried his face in my hair and groaned, giving in to his own release. Every muscle in his body shook and tensed as, just like I'd hoped, the windows let in enough light to illuminate the pleasure on his face. The utter ecstasy.

He collapsed on top of me, his arms holding tight. Our bodies were slick, sticky with sweat, as my heart pounded and the aftershocks pulsed.

Landon rolled off me, onto his back, then hauled me into his side. "That was just to take the edge off."

I smiled. If he wanted to repeat that all night long, I wouldn't object.

I was boneless. I was in the clouds. When Landon got up to deal with the condom, I barely moved. Not until he returned to the bed, pulling back the covers.

"You're bossy," I murmured as he lay down, once more placing me on his chest. "I like it."

"Good. Because we haven't even scratched the surface."

I curled deeper into his side.

He pressed his lips to my hair. "Sleep, Aubrey."

I hummed.

And fell asleep.

I stirred, lifting off my pillow—*why was it so firm?*—to glance at the clock. No, not a pillow. Landon.

Last night came rushing back as I held my breath, staring down at his handsome face.

The wedding. The orgasms. Oh God, the orgasms. Three. No, four. This man's body was built for sin. He'd woken me up twice in the night until after the last orgasm, when he'd made me come all over his tongue, I'd basically passed out.

I tore my eyes away from his soft lips and looked to the clock on the nightstand.

It was four in the morning. The sky outside was still dark. As much as I wanted to sleep for a few more hours, my mind was awake. So I slipped out of bed, tiptoeing to the en suite bathroom, where I eased the door closed and walked to the sink, taking a look at myself in the mirror.

My hair was a tangled mess. Last night's makeup was smudged beneath my eyes. I was sore in all the right places. My lips were swollen from Landon's mouth and my nipples were tender.

That man had thoroughly used my body last night. He'd taken control, and I'd loved it. I'd craved it.

I'd yielded to him without a moment's hesitation.

Was that why there was panic in my gaze as I stared in the mirror?

I didn't give up control. That was a great way to have your heart broken. My stomach churned. My heart beat too fast.

This was getting serious. Too serious. We barely knew each other. I still wasn't sure what exactly he wanted. Whatever it was, did I even have the capacity to give it?

How long would it take him to realize he wanted someone else?

Shit. My head was swimming. I needed . . . work. I needed the familiarity of emails and my fingers on a keyboard because it would chase away this anxious feeling. So I quietly collected some clothes from my walk-in closet, then escaped down the hall, taking a quick shower in the guest suite, before making myself some coffee in the kitchen and retreating to my office.

The moment I sat in my chair and splayed my hands across my desk, I expected to feel calm. Centered. Except that unease crept deeper until I felt close to puking.

I squeezed my eyes shut, breathing deeply, until the nausea passed. Then I shook my mouse, unlocked my computer and opened my inbox.

My fingers felt weak as I typed. Concentration was nearly impossible. But as I worked through email after email, my balance returned. The worries began to fade.

It was just sex, right? Phenomenal sex, but sex all the same. It didn't have to mean anything other than a physical release.

Landon and I were practically strangers. We had very different lives. He'd probably be the next in my string of failed relationships. That was okay. Maybe my problem all along was expecting something lasting.

Maybe if I just took this in bits, Landon wouldn't break—

"Hey, babe." He walked into my office with that lazy swagger. He'd pulled on his boxer briefs, the cotton straining at his bulky thighs. His washboard abs were on display and utterly mouthwatering.

I traced every line, every muscle, as he crossed the room. Then he bent to brush a kiss to my cheek. "What time is it?"

I glanced at my computer. "Four thirty."

He tucked a lock of damp hair behind my ear. "You okay?"

"Yeah," I lied.

"Good." He kissed my cheek again, then walked to the couch off to the side of the room.

It was the same white shade as the couches in my office. Most everything in my apartment was a shade of white or cream or gray.

I'd always preferred a modern, minimalist design. Every room in the house was simple, with clean lines. The rooms were bright, not a moody atmosphere to be found. It was the exact opposite of my mother's traditional style. She loved rich colors, smooth leather and plush carpets in elegant patterns.

This penthouse, like my office, had been my sanctuary. Except for the first time, it felt empty. Dull. Landon had to see that, didn't he? How boring it was?

He was a man who needed a homey space. A man

with character who was lying on a couch that lacked any sort of personality.

A chill crept across my skin, leaving goose bumps. When had my penthouse become so cold?

Landon yawned, picking up the throw that was tossed over the end of the couch. Then he covered himself up as he stretched out, his feet hanging over the end. "We're gonna need a bigger couch in here."

I blinked.

"Wake me up at six?"

"Um, sure." I nodded, waiting for him to tell me to stop working or to go back to bed.

But he just sighed and closed his eyes.

And fell back asleep.

This was too good to be true. It had to be.

What was I missing? There had to be something.

Whatever it was, I guess I'd find out when we fell apart. Because this would fall apart.

It always did.

fourteen

LANDON

AUBREY WAS SHUTTING ME OUT.

And it was pissing me the fuck off.

Had I heard from her since the wedding last weekend? Not a word. Had she bothered to return my texts? Nope. What the fuck did I have to do for my woman to pick up the goddamn phone and call me?

Apparently, it wasn't deliver orgasms.

She'd had four days of shutting me out. That ended. Now.

I stormed through the lobby on her floor at Kendrick Enterprises, not sparing the receptionist or Wilson a glance. "Is she in a meeting?" I asked Wynter when I reached her desk, not breaking my stride.

"No, but if you just give me a moment, I can let her know you're here."

"Oh, I'll tell her myself." I passed her desk and ripped open Aubrey's door.

She was seated at her desk, eyes on her phone. When I marched inside, her face whipped up, her mouth parting.

"So you didn't lose your phone." I scowled and stopped in front of her desk, planting my fists on my hips.

"I've been busy." She set her phone down.

"Did I ask you to stop being busy?"

"No. But I don't have a job where I can just walk away at the end of my shift. I get caught up."

"Again, did I ask you to stop getting caught up?"

She swallowed hard. "No."

"Don't do this, Aubrey."

She met my gaze, not needing me to explain. We both knew I was calling her on this bullshit.

"Are you done with meetings for the day?" I asked.

"Yes, but—"

"I'm hungry," I cut her off before she could protest. "What do you want for dinner?"

"I can't—"

"Pizza? Great. Me too. Beer or wine or water?"

"I don't—"

"Wine. Good call. Something red."

"You're not listening to me." She stood from her chair, her hands balling at the sides of her simple black dress.

"No, I'm not listening to you. Not when you're about to say something to push me away."

"I need to concentrate." Aubrey crossed her arms

over her chest, and damn it, that glare she sent my way just made me want to kiss her.

"Then concentrate." I waved to her computer, spun around and stormed out of her office as quickly as I'd come inside.

Wynter's eyes bugged out as I strode past her desk for the elevator.

But I ignored her, I ignored everyone, as I made my way to the first floor, then walked three blocks to the closest pizzeria. I ordered a medium pepperoni and snagged a bottle of wine, tipping the clerk before I strode back outside and into the December cold.

Balancing the pizza box in one hand with the wine tucked beneath my arm, I fished my phone from a pocket and hit Aubrey's name.

"Hello," she answered.

"Do you have a corkscrew? Plates? Napkins?"

"Landon—"

"Yes or no."

She blew out a long breath. "Yes."

I ended the call and stomped to her building. The pizza wouldn't be hot, not with today's freezing temperatures, but as I rode up the elevator, it was still warm enough.

It was after six by the time the elevator doors opened, and the receptionist was gone from her desk. Wilson had moved to stand beside Wynter's now-empty desk.

"I'll take her home," I told Wilson. "I get it if you

want to stay. Respect, man. But you've got help. I won't let anything happen to her, and I'm sure as fuck not going to hurt her."

He studied me for a few long moments, then nodded. Apparently, I'd passed Wilson's test.

"Have a good night," I said, pushing into Aubrey's office.

She was behind her desk, fingers on her keyboard. The click of her typing stopped as I walked toward the couches.

Without a word, I set the pizza on the coffee table along with the wine bottle, then went to the small kitchenette just off her private bathroom.

I took out plates, forks, napkins and two crystal wineglasses. I rifled through drawers until I found a corkscrew. Then I returned to the office, Aubrey's eyes on me as I moved. I plated her pizza first and poured her a glass of cabernet, taking her dinner to her desk.

"Thank you," she murmured.

"Welcome." I returned to the couch, taking off my coat before fixing my own plate. I scrolled through my phone as I ate and sipped from my wine. When I was finished, I collected her dishes and my own, taking them to the kitchenette to wash and clean up.

Aubrey's gaze flicked my way as I moved, but I didn't say a word as I returned to the couch, toeing off my shoes and stretching out. My legs were too long and my feet were sticking off the end, just like the sofa in her home office.

The click of Aubrey's nails on her keyboard filled the silence. I sent a few texts, checking in on Lacy before I replied to Baldwin, who wanted to meet up this weekend for a beer.

And finally, after an hour—after I wasn't as angry as I'd been—I texted Aubrey. Her phone dinged on her desk.

We need to have a conversation about your couches. They're too small.

"I'll get longer couches."

I grinned, my fingers typing out another message.

Come here.

The wheels of her chair rolled over the floor before her heels clicked and she stopped by my head.

I jackknifed to a seat, crooking my finger, guiding her to stand between my legs. I put my hands on her hips, my thumbs massaging small circles. "Did you get enough to eat?"

"Yes." Her hand came to my hair, her fingers threading through the strands.

I pulled her down so she was seated on my lap and her gaze was level with my own. "Hi."

Her eyes softened. "Hi."

"You will always have my support. You can run your empire. I'll never try to take that from you. But don't put it between us because you're scared."

Her chin dropped, her shoulders slumped. "I don't know what you want from me."

"You." I took her face in a hand, tilting it up. "Just you."

Aubrey searched my eyes, like she was expecting to find a lie.

I blamed that shit on Abel and the other fuckheads who'd come before me. But she'd see. In time, she'd see.

"Sorry," she whispered.

I took her mouth, sealing my lips over hers and sweeping my tongue across her lower lip. I'd never get enough of how she felt. The soft pout. The sweet whimper whenever I tangled my tongue with hers. I kissed her until she was breathless. Until the tension crept from her frame.

"Missed you." I dropped my forehead to hers.

She closed her eyes, nodding. Then she bit her bottom lip, giving me a wicked smile.

"What?"

She shifted off my lap and stood, then sauntered to the door, flipping the lock.

One little click and I was instantly hard.

Aubrey returned, standing before me. She held out a hand, so I stood, expecting her to lead me somewhere. But then she dropped to her knees. "I want to do something."

Fuck. Yes. Her hands came to my jeans, and with a flick, the button was undone. She slid the zipper free, then tugged at the hem, dragging the denim down my thighs along with the boxer briefs beneath.

She moaned, fitting her hand around my shaft.

"Fuck, babe." I tipped my head back as she stroked, and when her tongue licked along the underside of my cock, I nearly came apart.

Aubrey took me in her mouth, hot and wet. *Heaven*. She sucked, hard, and licked the pearly drop of come at the tip. Then another wicked grin before she swallowed me down.

My fingers dove into her hair, holding her as I fucked her mouth. She was a damn miracle, this woman. Her mouth was a fucking dream, and she was relentless, working me until I was on the verge of losing control. So I eased her away, waiting until she looked up beneath those sooty lashes.

"You're on your knees but you own me. You like that, don't you, sweetheart?"

"Yes," she whispered.

"See what power you have over me?" I fisted my cock, dragging the head across her lips. "You can have power over me every fucking day. But don't shut me out."

Aubrey opened, about to take me again, but I reached down and hauled her to her feet. Then in a spin that made her yelp, I had her back on the couch.

"My turn." I grinned and shoved up the skirt of her dress, revealing those sexy legs and a pair of lace panties I would gladly tear from her body.

"Landon," she warned.

I tugged. *Rip*.

"Those were from Paris."

The frown she sent me disappeared with a moan as I dove in, dragging my tongue through her soaked center. I flicked her clit, earning a gasp, and savored that sweet taste, feasting as I drove her up and up and up.

"Oh my God, Landon." Aubrey writhed, her hand fisting my hair, but before she could come, I dove into my pocket for a condom, hustling to sheathe myself.

My shirt was yanked over my head. My jeans kicked to the floor. I fumbled to find the zipper on her dress and pull it over her head. As it sailed to the floor, I positioned at her entrance and thrust home.

"Fuck," I cursed, clenching my teeth so I wouldn't make a damn fool of myself.

Her legs wrapped around my hips. Those heels of hers digging into my ass.

I rolled my hips, sliding deeper until I earned a gasp. Her breasts were perfect, wrapped in lace. I took a nipple in my mouth, and even through the bra, I felt it pebble on my tongue as Aubrey's inner walls fluttered.

Then we fucked, desperately. Like the past four days had been a nightmare and I'd finally walked into the light.

"Every day. You're mine, every day." I wasn't going without her again.

"Yes," she cried, and when I reached between us

to find her clit, she detonated, her back arching off the couch.

The build at the base of my spine, the tightening in every muscle, reached its peak and I followed on a groan, my entire body trembling as I roared through my release, collapsing when I was drained.

The condom needed to be dealt with, but I couldn't leave this couch. Not yet. The haze cleared and I lifted, not wanting to crush her, and spun us around so she was lying on my chest. I wrapped her in my arms, willing whatever worries she had in that beautiful head to vanish.

This woman . . . I'd been in a shit mood this week. No surprise why. So I held her tighter.

Fuck, but this was good. So fucking good. How could she not want this? Didn't she feel this connection? This intensity? You didn't walk away from something like this. You didn't turn your back on the potential of what this could be.

"You're right." She pushed up on an elbow, her hair cascading around her face, the ends tickling my bare chest.

"About?"

"This couch is too small."

I smiled, and for the first time in days, that knot in my gut loosened. So I rolled us to the floor.

Where we had plenty of space for round two.

fifteen

Aubrey

"Morning, babe." Landon strolled into the kitchen, buttoning yesterday's shirt.

"Morning." I slid a cup of coffee across the counter.

He lifted the mug, taking a sip, before coming to my side and pulling me closer. His lips came to my hair for a kiss.

Beneath the scent of my own bodywash, that addictive cologne lingered from yesterday. I breathed him in. *Be real. Please.*

After last night, when he'd barged into my office angry and frustrated, I'd been sure it was over. But he'd stayed. He'd brought me dinner and just hung out while I'd finished working. Then after sex on the couch—and the floor—we'd come to my place and crashed.

"Are you working today?" I asked.

"Yeah." He took another sip of coffee. "I need to run home. Get my uniform. Head to the precinct."

"Want a ride?"

He looked over my head at the dark windows, where it was snowing. It had started last night as we'd driven here and must not have stopped. The streets and sidewalks would be a mess. "That would be great. What time—"

Before he could finish his sentence, his phone vibrated in his pocket.

Landon let me go and pulled it out, frowning at the screen. "Give me one minute?"

"Of course." I nodded, watching as he retreated down the hallway.

Be real.

I took a sip of my own coffee, glancing at the microwave. It was five thirty, and given the snow, I'd asked Glen to come ten minutes earlier than normal. He'd be here shortly. I had a call with a company in London starting at six thirty, and I wanted to be in the office early to prepare.

So I took my mug and headed out of the kitchen to collect my laptop from my office. But Landon's voice stopped me before I went too far.

"I know I'm behind on this month's payment. I'm getting the money. I just need another week. Please."

I froze. My stomach dropped. *Money.*

Money. Money. Money.

That word ran through my mind on loop as my knees nearly buckled.

I knew it. I knew this was too good to be true.

I'd asked him about my money and he'd made a joke. He'd laughed it off. And I'd fallen for it.

I'd fallen, unquestionably.

"How much do you need?" Landon asked, his voice low. "Okay. I'll, um . . . I'll bring you a check after work."

Move. Walk away, Aubrey. But my feet were glued to the floor, next to my splashed heart.

Damn it. This hurt. It shouldn't hurt. Landon and I were . . . what were we?

We were a possibility. We were a dream. We were the promise of greatness.

And now it was over.

My hand was shaking, a drop of coffee sloshing over and landing by my shoe. I turned, ready to retreat to the kitchen for a towel, but stopped when he spoke a name. A woman's name.

"Tell Lacy I love her. And that I'll see her later today, okay?"

Lacy.

Who was Lacy?

"Bye." Landon ended the call and sighed. "Fuck."

It was too late for me to escape. He was too close. So I blanked my expression and squared my shoulders. I assumed the face I wore in negotiations. Thank God I'd had years to practice. I took a sip of my coffee, swallowing the lump in my throat, then walked down the hallway like I'd just left the kitchen.

Landon met me in the hallway, his forehead furrowed.

"I just need to grab my laptop, then I'll be ready."

"Okay." He nodded, tucking his phone away.

I walked, shoulders straight and chin held high, like there wasn't a hole in my chest.

At least I knew, right? At least this ended now, instead of in months or years. Instead of after I'd fallen in love with him.

Or was it too late?

This was all my fault. I'd sworn off men, and the moment a handsome guy had strolled into my office, my vow had been tossed in the trash.

How could I have been so gullible? So stupid?

Every beat of my heart was pained. My nose stung and my eyes flooded as I walked into the office. But I wiped them dry, refusing to let myself cry. Not yet.

I'd cry after I told Landon I never wanted to see him again.

This morning, I had to get to work. Where it was safe. So I collected my things and walked to the entryway for a coat.

Landon was waiting, his own coat covering his broad shoulders. "You okay?"

"Good," I lied.

"Aubrey." He took my chin, forcing me to meet his gaze. "What's wrong?"

Wrong? Everything. Everything was wrong. I'd trusted him. Believed him. Wanted him.

And I'd been a fool.

"Who's Lacy?" I hated the crack in my voice. "Was it always about my money?"

"What the fuck?" He dropped his hand like my skin was on fire. Then he made a T with his hands. "Time out. Stop the clock. Say that again."

"My money. Is that why you're here?"

The hurt in his gaze was like a knife jabbed through my ribs. His expression morphed in a flash, pain to anger. His jaw clenched and his nostrils flared. Then he held up one finger.

And used it to stab the button for the elevator.

The seconds it took for the doors to open were excruciating. I held my breath, willing it to come faster. Then finally, a chime and it opened, ready to sweep him away.

"What kind of man do you think I am, Aubrey?" Landon's voice was quiet. Calm. "Will you ever stop comparing me to the assholes in your past? Or have I always been doomed to fail?"

A tear dripped down my cheek as he strode into the elevator. Then he was gone, without a backward glance.

Another tear fell. Then another.

"Fuck." I wiped my eyes dry just as my phone rang in my tote, making me jump. I frantically dug it out. Glen's name flashed on the screen with a text that he'd arrived. I sniffled and wiped my eyes dry, then grabbed a coat and hit the button for the elevator.

My chin quivered the entire ride to the first floor and

the slow drive to work. I scanned the sidewalks, hoping I'd see Landon walking, but there was no sign of him.

What kind of man do you think I am, Aubrey?

Will you ever stop comparing me to the assholes in your past?

He was right. Of course he was right. I'd been holding everything against him, waiting for him to fail. And instead, it had been me who'd been the failure.

What the hell was wrong with me?

I hadn't even asked about the call. I'd just made an assumption.

The wrong assumption.

I tapped my foot on the SUV's floor, willing us to get to the office quicker. I wanted to call Landon but didn't want Glen to overhear, and by the time I raised the partition, we'd be minutes away. Not enough time for me to apologize. To grovel.

No, I wanted to make this call in my office. But the moment I stepped off the private elevator, Wynter was already waiting with a fistful of sticky notes.

Maybe it was better to give Landon time anyway. I'd call him in an hour, after he'd had time to get to work. Except meeting bled into meeting, eating up my morning. The hours ticked by painfully, and every time I thought I had a spare minute to call Landon, someone interrupted me.

Five minutes. I just wanted five minutes. Instead, I sat

in a conference room, listening to one of my senior vice presidents talk about our year-end financial projections.

Was this really going to be my life? Unable to find five minutes for myself? For Landon?

"Excuse me." I stood from my chair abruptly, drawing attention from the entire room. "Something has come up and I need to duck out. Can you please let Wynter know if there's anything urgent?"

My CFO, Matt, nodded. "Everything is on target. This was just a recap."

Then why the hell had we been sitting here for an hour?

I strode from the conference room, nodding for Wynter to follow as I hurried down the hallway to my office. "Find time with Matt next week. That meeting was a waste of everyone's time. Especially mine. An email would have sufficed."

"Yes, Ms. Kendrick." She scribbled on her pad of Post-its.

"I want you to start being more selective about meetings after five. Unless it's an emergency, it will have to wait."

"Oh, um, okay." Up until today, I'd never once told her to back off on scheduling. From six in the morning until seven at night, I'd been entirely available.

Too available.

Maybe because I hadn't wanted to face the facts. The

men in my past had expected me to bend. To be someone else.

Landon had never asked me to change. He didn't expect it or need it.

Which was why I'd change. Because it was my choice. Because what I wanted more than anything else at the moment, even my career, was Landon.

If it wasn't too late.

"I need a few minutes alone before lunch," I told Wynter, rounding the corner. But as my office door came into view, so did a man wearing a police uniform.

My feet stuttered. I recovered quickly, blanking my face. "Officer Bertello. Nice to see you again."

"Ms. Kendrick." He nodded. "May I have a moment?"

I forced a tight smile. "Not without my lawyer present."

"That probably won't be necessary. Maybe I could have five to explain. Then you can call in the lawyer."

"Fine." So much for five minutes to myself. I walked to my office door, opening it and waving him inside.

Wynter took a step like she was going to retreat to her desk, but I shook my head. "Listen in, please."

"Of course." She scurried past me, following Officer Bertello to the couches.

I glanced toward the lobby, wishing there was a different police officer in the building.

Wilson abandoned his post beside Leah's desk and marched for my office. "I'll sit in too."

"Thank you." I sighed, then joined Bertello and Wynter, taking the couch where Landon and I had been last night.

Never again would I sit here and not think of his face as he'd thrust inside me. That was the way it would be forever, wouldn't it? If I bought larger couches, would he be around to help me use them?

"Ms. Kendrick."

I blinked, tearing my eyes away from the upholstery. "Yes."

"Just a quick update for you today. No questions." Officer Bertello took out his notepad and flipped to a page. "Last time I was here, I asked you about a ring you'd purchased."

"For five thousand dollars."

He nodded. "That's right. In cash."

I crossed my legs, placing my hands together on my lap.

"A young man sold that ring to you."

"Yes."

"An employee of the shop owner. He was the one who reported the theft to the owner."

"There was no theft." My molars ground together.

"According to the owner of the shop, the man came to her. Said you and your father came into the shop to look at two rings. He took out the trays and boxes, giving you time to browse. It was as he was putting everything away, after you'd left, that he noticed two rings were missing."

That little shit. As suspected, he'd either lied to his boss, the shop's owner, or they'd concocted this scam together.

"Did you know the shop owner isn't the building owner?" Bertello asked.

"No. I've only been the one time."

"Ah. Well, the shop owner didn't realize that the building owner installed some surveillance cameras on the exterior. There happened to be one mounted on a corner, and if you watch it at just the right angle, you can see the shop's front door."

I arched my eyebrows, waiting for him to continue.

"I couldn't see you, other than when you came in and left. But afterward, that young man walked to the door. Probably to check that you were really gone. And you know what he put in his pocket?"

"Cash?"

"The shop owner reported it, believing her employee. But we arrested him earlier this week. Apologies for not getting you an update sooner. I, uh, well, it took me a bit to track down the footage. With the holiday thrown in . . ."

"It's fine." It wasn't fine, but I was relieved enough to lie. "I appreciate you coming over today."

He returned the notepad to his coat pocket, then

stood, glancing around the office. "Nice office. I received an interesting call after my last visit here."

"Oh?" I stood.

"Officer Landon McClellan. A good buddy of his, Bo Baldwin, works with me in Chelsea." The corners of Bertello's mouth turned up. "He *encouraged* me to be thorough. Got the sense that if I buggered this one up, he'd help make my life a living hell."

My heart. I really, *really* needed to talk to Landon. I needed these people out of my office so I could apologize.

"Out of curiosity," Bertello said, "do you happen to have that ring in your safe? I've been wondering what it looks like. Got a sketch but . . . would you mind?"

Yes. Yes, I would mind. "Not at all," I lied again. "One moment."

My heels pounded on the floor, as loud as my heartbeat, as I hurried past the bathroom and into the closet, keying in the code to my safe, more than ready to appease this cop and get him the hell out of my building.

But as the safe's door swung open, my heart stopped.

Empty.

The entire thing was empty.

I patted the surface, like it was an illusion. But that ring was gone. So was the three thousand dollars I kept inside.

"Oh my God." I checked again, spinning in a circle to look around the floor, like maybe that ring had magically crawled out.

But it was gone.

I backed away from the safe, my heart hammering. Where was the ring? Where was the money?

I turned and jogged into the office, moving straight for my phone that I'd left on the couch.

"Ms. Kendrick?" Wynter asked, but I held up a hand, unlocking the phone to hit one name and press it to my ear.

"Aubrey, I'm busy."

"Landon."

"What's wrong?" He heard the panic in my voice. "Where are you?"

"Work."

"Hang tight." He didn't hesitate. "Be right there."

sixteen

LANDON

I HURRIED OFF THE ELEVATOR, RUSHING TO AUBREY'S OFFICE. There was a clump of snow on my boot from the walk over, and it skidded across the smooth floor.

Wynter wasn't at her desk. Wilson wasn't at his usual post. So I walked faster, practically jogging as I shoved through her office door.

Aubrey stood in the center of the room, her bottom lip worried between her teeth.

Another cop was sitting on a couch. It had to be Bertello. Was that why she'd called?

The moment I walked inside, Aubrey spun around, her eyes wide and face pale.

Wynter was standing against the window, eyes locked on her boss. Wilson was beside the couch, positioned between Bertello and Aubrey.

Instead of asking Aubrey what was going on, I walked straight into her space, took her elbow and steered her to the en suite, kicking the door closed behind us as we disappeared.

I stopped when we reached the kitchenette. "What's wrong? I'm assuming that's Bertello. Why didn't you call the lawyer?"

"It's not about Bertello." Aubrey took my hand and dragged me into the closet, stopping beside an open safe. "Bertello came to tell me that the ring he suspected we stole was in fact not stolen. The guy who worked at the antique shop kept the money and told the owner we stole it when he wasn't looking."

"Okay," I drawled. "That's good news."

"No, it's not good news. Because Bertello asked me to see the ring out of curiosity, and I came in here to get it and it's gone." Her voice began to rise, the panic I'd heard on the phone clearer now. "Everything's gone. Including some cash I had in here too."

"When was the last time you checked the safe?"

"When I showed it to you the last time Bertello was here. It's been weeks."

"Who has access to the safe? Who knows the combination?"

"Just my dad." She wrapped her arms around her stomach. "That's it."

"Come here." I pulled her into my chest, holding tight as she sagged against me. Even though I was still pissed about what she'd said this morning, I couldn't be this close to her, see her this upset, and not touch her. "Okay, let's start by calling your dad."

She nodded, standing tall and opening her phone. She hit his name and put him on speaker.

"Hi," he answered. "How are you today?"

"Dad, did you come into my office and open my safe?"

"Yes, earlier this morning. You were in a meeting."

Her entire body sagged and her eyes closed. "You didn't tell me that. I thought someone came into my office and broke in."

"I wrote you a sticky note," he said. "Left it on your assistant's desk."

She sighed. "I'm assuming you took the cash I had in here too."

"Yeah, sorry. I forgot my wallet again, and I'm on my way to a lunch meeting. Also on the sticky note."

Aubrey rubbed at a temple. "It must have gotten lost in the shuffle."

Probably because her assistant loved sticky notes.

I shook my head, letting my own panic fade. When she'd called, I'd been in the middle of a meeting with my boss, trying to work out a schedule for the next month that accommodated my side job. But she'd called and I'd bolted, racing here and riding the adrenaline.

My heart climbed out of my throat.

And a smile tugged at my mouth.

"Okay, Dad. Thanks."

"Do you have any free time later?" he asked. "Swing by my office."

"Sure."

No, Aubrey didn't have free time. I could see her mentally shuffling her schedule, trying to find an available minute.

"Bye." She ended the call, her shoulders sagging. "I'm such an idiot. I panicked and didn't even think to call him. I'm a freaking mess today. I'm screwing everything up."

I put my hands on her shoulders. "You're not an idiot."

"Are you sure about that? Maybe replay this morning and you'll change your mind."

I chuckled, framing her face with my hands and tipping it back so I could see those pretty brown eyes. "You called me."

"Sorry. I'm sure you were busy and didn't have time to rush over here because I'm falling apart."

"You called me."

"I know and I'm sorr—"

"Aubrey. Stop." I ran a thumb over her cheek. "I've been waiting months for you to finally call me. This is the first time that my phone rang with your name on the screen."

"What? No, it's not. I've called you."

I arched my eyebrows, watching as those gears in her marvelous mind turned.

"That can't be right. I really haven't called you before?"

I shook my head, laughing and hauling her into my chest again. "It only took a slight nonemergency."

"Well . . . who else would I call?" she whispered, wrapping her arms around my waist. "Landon, I'm sorry. I'm so sorry for what I said earlier."

I dropped my cheek to her hair. "Let's get rid of the people in your office. Then we'll talk."

She nodded, but her arms tightened, like she wasn't ready to let go.

So I held her until she was, then followed her to the office, hovering close while she explained.

"Just a bit of a misunderstanding," she said. "Officer Bertello, my dad came to pick up the ring today to have it wrapped for my mother. Sorry."

"No problem." He stood, nodding to her before he looked at me. "Landon McClellan?"

I nodded. "Yep. If you're going back to the precinct, say hello to Baldwin for me."

"Will do," Bertello said. "I'll see myself out, Ms. Kendrick."

Aubrey waited until he was gone, then she went to a couch—our couch—sagging on its edge. "Wynter, would you mind clearing my lunch hour? And I need an hour later today to meet with my father."

"Of course," Wynter said. "Anything else?"

"No, thank you. Thanks, Wilson." She gave him a small smile, then watched as they left.

I shrugged off my coat and draped it over an arm of the couch. Then I took the space at Aubrey's side, leaning my elbows to my knees.

"You seem too good to be true," she said.

"I'm not."

"You never complain about my hours. You don't care when I take calls or answer emails while we're at dinner. You don't tell me to stop working or to put my phone away. Why?"

"Because that's part of you." I shifted, facing her, and hooked a finger under her chin so she could see the truth in my face. "I'm not going to ask you to change, Aubrey. You work because you love it. Why would I take that from you? I know that when you're done, you'll come to me. I'll be there. I can live with that. Can you?"

Her eyes flooded. "What is wrong with me? It's like I'm trying to sabotage this. Like I'm purposefully trying to fail."

"There is no fail here, sweetheart. Not as long as we walk out of this together."

She sniffled and leaned in, letting her forehead crash against my chest. Then she crawled into my lap, burrowing deep. "I'm sorry."

"Make it up to me. Buy me a bigger couch."

Aubrey laughed, the sweet sound soothing away any lingering anger.

"About what you heard earlier," I said.

"You don't have to tell me. I shouldn't have eavesdropped."

No, it was time to share. I'd kept Lacy close to my chest for a lot of reasons. But if there was ever a person who I wanted to know about my past, it was Aubrey.

"Lacy is my sister."

Aubrey sat up straight. "Oh. I didn't realize you had a sister."

"She's ten years younger," I said. "She turned twenty-five in October. Lacy wasn't planned. My parents didn't think they could have other kids, then, surprise."

Lacy had joined our family like she'd been the piece we hadn't even realized was missing. Smart. Charming. Her laugh would brighten the darkest of days.

"When my mom was diagnosed with cancer, it hit Dad the hardest. Lacy too. I was working, but Lacy was living at home, trying to help out while she was taking classes at a community college."

"That must have been hard."

"It was. But she smiled through it all. A ray of endless sunshine. That's who she was."

"Was?" Aubrey didn't miss much.

"My mom died two years ago. It was devastating, especially for Dad. We all had a hard time climbing out of our grief, but especially Dad. Hell, he didn't even try. But Lacy, she was determined to get him through it. She hardly left his side. For months, she didn't leave him. One night, she called me crying. It was just too much. She needed a break."

I'd replayed that phone call a thousand times. Each time, I wished I had handled it differently.

"She asked if she could bring Dad to my place. Just to get him out of the house. To get him out of the bed where Mom . . ."

"Landon." Aubrey took my hand between hers.

"Lacy was driving. Dad was in the passenger seat. A drunk driver ran a red light, T-boned their car. The other driver died on impact. So did Dad."

Aubrey gasped. "Oh my God. I'm so sorry."

There were over ten thousand deaths a year from drunk drivers. Approximately one death every fifty-two minutes. Those were the hardest cases for me as a cop, pulling over a driver who'd been drinking, especially those who bitched when I hauled them to jail and said it was no big deal.

It was a big fucking deal. A man who'd had three glasses of wine with dinner and had chosen to drive home had killed my father. And had destroyed my sister's life.

"Lacy suffered severe head trauma. She'll, um . . . the doctors say she'll never recover. She's not the person she was. Most days, she doesn't know who she is. The bad days, she does. She remembers who she used to be. And who she's become. She's in a home because she needs round-the-clock care."

"That's who you were talking to this morning," Aubrey said.

I nodded. "It's expensive. Mom's treatment was expensive. And Dad had life insurance, but it only covers part of things. The rest is up to me. There are cheaper places, but she's my sister. She's comfortable where she's at and I like the nursing staff. So I make it work. I take on private security jobs when I'm not at the precinct because they pay."

"You do private security? Like Wilson?"

"Yeah. You know that gym where we ran into each other? The owner is a guy who hired me to help at this fancy event he was hosting. He gave me the gym membership as a perk. And he's been trying to hire me full-time."

"But you love being a cop."

"I love my sister more." I gave her a sad smile. "For now, I can manage both. If that changes, then I'll turn in my badge."

Aubrey traced her fingers over my face, then stood and walked to the windows. "I can help."

"Not why I'm telling you."

"I know. But what's the point of all this?" She tossed a hand in the air. "What's the point if I can't help?"

I stood and walked over. "Appreciate it, babe. But I won't accept."

"That's ridiculous." She scoffed.

"Maybe. Except it is what it is. If we get to the point

where we share an address, we'll have that conversation. But not yet."

"You think we'll get to that point?"

"Fuck, I hope so." I'd spend my life drowning in her beautiful eyes. Letting her throw that sass in my face.

"I hope so too," she whispered.

If time stopped when we were together, like it had for weeks, we'd have all the time in the world to get to that point. To the point where she had more than this job. Where I had more than a broken family.

I just wished my mother, my father, had been able to meet Aubrey. That Aubrey had been able to know Lacy before.

But some wishes weren't meant to come true. So I wished harder for those that might.

I bent and dropped a kiss to her mouth, lingering until her lipstick was smudged. "I want nothing from you but your heart."

"Maybe you already have it."

Maybe I did. She sure as hell had mine. "Don't plan on me giving it back."

epilogue

Charlie

Nine years later . . .

"I remember the night Landon proposed to you," I told Aunt Aubrey. "It was at the bar."

"On New Year's Eve, about a year after we started dating. We came to Montana for Christmas."

"I remember your wedding too." I'd been her flower girl. "I remember walking into your office, and there were so many cops."

Aubrey laughed, holding up her left hand. The summer sunshine caught the solitaire diamond ring on her finger. It was modest, not something you'd expect for a woman worth millions. But it was her. And it was Uncle Landon.

Much like how Mom's ring was striking in its simplicity. Dad could afford to buy her enough diamonds to fill his boat, but all Mom wanted was a beautiful jewel that fit into her everyday life.

"Your uncle thought getting married in the office

was so clever and hilarious," Aubrey said. "His rationale was that since I'd been married to my job for so long, he didn't want me and work to break up. Instead, he'd just share me with the office. What better way than to get married there?"

The details were fuzzy but I recalled the dress Mom had forced me to wear along with curling my hair. But she'd compromised and let me wear my tennis shoes instead of fancy slippers. The second the ceremony had wrapped up, I'd pulled on the Lark Cove Bar hat I'd stashed in my backpack.

Aubrey and Landon's wedding had been my first visit to the Kendrick Enterprises building. Before that trip, we'd spent most of our New York vacations exploring the city and staying at my parents' penthouse in Manhattan. That, or we'd gone to my grandparents' estate in Oyster Bay on Long Island.

Even now, I hadn't spent much time at Kendrick Enterprises. But I'd never forget her office. I'd been mesmerized by the windows overlooking the city. As Aubrey and Landon had exchanged vows in front of an arched altar weaved with flowers and greenery, I'd sat in my chair and stared through those windows.

"I was pregnant with Greyson," Aubrey said. "And terrified I'd puke all over Landon's tux or on my dress."

"That was a pretty dress." Not that I remembered it from that day, but Mom had a gallery wall upstairs. "Your ex. That lawyer. Abel. What happened with him?"

"Nothing." She shrugged. "He went about his life. I went about mine. I cut back at work, not because Landon asked me to, but because I wanted to. We found a balance together. Abel and I bump into each other now and again for work. But that heartbreak, it was just a blip on the radar."

"I want to get to that point." To the point where Dustin Lewis was nothing but a footnote. An unpleasant memory.

"You will," Aubrey promised.

I stared out over the lake. Dad's boat crossed the bay, returning home. "I didn't know about Landon's sister."

"He doesn't talk about Lacy much."

"Is she, um . . ." *Alive*. I couldn't bring myself to say the word.

"She lives in a home. After we got engaged, Landon finally let me start paying for her care. We moved her to a nice place with more space and personalized nurses. We visit as often as we can. The boys know who she is. Sometimes there are minor improvements, but they are rare. We just love her. That's all we can do."

My heart twisted.

Aubrey sat up straighter as the boat slowed and approached the dock.

Dad eased it into its spot as Landon hopped out, tying it up. Then the rest of the crew piled out, the kids all racing for the house.

"Charlie, we're going shoreline picking," Camila said as her footsteps pounded across the deck. "Wanna come?"

"Sure." I smiled.

Shoreline picking was Mom's version of art supply shopping. We'd take a long walk along the lake, searching for any trash that might have washed up or been tossed out. She'd find treasures in that trash and turn it into art.

"We're going fishing." Collin bounded up the deck's stairs with Greyson and Bodie running to keep up. They were all dripping wet.

"Hi, Mom!" Greyson giggled as he bolted into the house. "Bye, Mom!"

Bodie veered by Aubrey's chair and gave her a quick kiss. Then he chased the older boys inside.

Mom was next, carrying a bunch of wet towels. "Did Camila tell you we're going shoreline picking?"

"Yeah." I nodded. "I'm coming too."

"Me too," Aubrey said.

"Oh, good." Mom smiled. "I'll get buckets. And those claw grabber things your dad bought me."

"Mom! Can we have a snack?" Collin yelled from inside.

"Yes," she hollered back and disappeared into the house.

Dad came to the deck railing. "We're going fishing. Want to come?"

"I'm going with Mom and Camila."

"Good. How are you feeling?"

I looked at Aubrey, her gaze waiting. "I'll be all right."

Dad exhaled, like he'd been waiting for that reassurance. Then he shoved away from the deck, rounding the house for the garage.

Landon walked up the stairs, coming to Aubrey's chaise. "Hi, babe."

"Hi. How was boating?"

"Fun. The boys are going to hit you up later. They think we should add another week to our vacation."

She laughed. "I was thinking the same thing."

"Yeah?"

"I'll have to work here and there, keep up on emails, but I can swing it. I wouldn't mind another week."

"This is the perk of early retirement, Charlie." Landon leaned in to kiss his wife. "Ultimate flexibility."

Uncle Landon had retired from the police force around the time Bodie had turned one. According to Dad, Landon had been working long hours, and combined with Aubrey's demanding schedule, the boys had been spending most of their time with a nanny.

One day, Landon had come home from his shift and the nanny had told him that Bodie had taken his first steps.

Both Landon and Aubrey had missed it.

So he'd retired. He stayed home with his sons, and as far as I could tell, he had no regrets.

"Sorry about the cheating asshole," Landon said, giving me a warm smile.

"Yeah, me too."

"It takes a strong man to love a Kendrick woman. Remember that, Charlie."

"I will."

He winked at me, kissed Aubrey again, then stood and went inside, likely to round up the boys for fishing.

"I don't know what's next," I told Aubrey. "I'd planned to get a job in Bozeman. To fit my life around Dustin's. Now what?"

"Maybe something new?"

"Like what?"

"My assistant, Wynter, is leaving at the end of the summer. Well, not leaving. She's getting promoted. So I need a new assistant. What do you say?"

I sat up straighter. "Me?"

"Why not?"

Why not?

Aubrey shifted, swinging her legs over the side of the chair. "You could try it for a year. Live in your dad's penthouse."

Leave Montana? Work for Aubrey? In New York City? "Are you seriously offering me a job?"

"I'm offering you a different perspective. Think about it." She stood, ready to head inside. But before she could open the door, I stopped her.

"Aubrey?"

"Yeah?"

"Thank you for telling me your story."

"Anytime."

I looked to the lake as she disappeared inside. Lark Cove was home. It would always be home.

But maybe it was time to stretch my wings. To fly a little farther.

A smile tugged at my mouth.

New York City.

An adventure.

Why not?

BONUS *epilogue*

CHARLIE

Three years later . . .

I TIPTOED THROUGH MOM AND DAD'S QUIET HOUSE, TRYING not to wake anyone as I made my way to the kitchen. Outside, the robins chirped. The sun had just peeked over the mountains, the horizon a golden glow tinged with pink. The rays creeped through the house as I padded out of my childhood bedroom, in desperate need of some caffeine.

I was halfway down the staircase when the aroma of fresh coffee caught my nose.

Dad was waiting for me in the kitchen, standing beside a full coffee pot.

"So much for being the first one up," I said, my voice low.

"Morning, peanut." He held out a steaming mug. "Figured you'd still be on Eastern time."

"What's your excuse for getting up so early?" I took a careful sip so I didn't scald my tongue.

"I'm just happy you're home."

"Me too."

For good.

I'd spent the past three years in New York. The different perspective Aubrey had offered me had changed my life.

But three years in the city had been enough for my country heart. Montana had called me home.

I'd flown in yesterday afternoon, though the majority of my belongings were still in shipping boxes bound for Lark Cove.

They'd stay in those boxes for a while until I determined my next step. Maybe I'd stay in Lark Cove. Maybe I'd find a new town to call home.

I was on the precipice of another adventure, and though the unknown was nerve-racking, this morning, I was simply going to enjoy being home.

Dad and I drank our coffee in silence, content to be in each other's company.

I'd come home for holidays over the past three years. Mom and Dad had taken trips to visit the city. But this was different because there was no time limit. No dread at the end of a vacation.

"What's the plan for today?" I asked Dad.

"Camila has a birthday party to go to," Dad said. "But otherwise, no plans. Figured you might want to have a day to hang out. We can go have dinner at the bar. There are a lot of people who are glad to have you home. Sofia, Dakota and the kids are coming over later."

"Sounds perfect."

He refilled his mug, then held out the pot to fill mine as well.

"I might go for a walk this morning. Before everyone wakes up."

"Good idea." He set his mug down to retrieve an empty one from the cupboard. "I'm going to take your mom some coffee."

"Okay." I went over and gave him a hug, then stood to kiss his cheek. "I love you, Dad."

"I love you too, peanut."

"See you in a bit." I walked to the sliding doors that led to the deck, finding a pair of Mom's clogs outside. I slid them on, then zipped up my hoodie, taking the path that curved around the edge of the bay.

The cool air seeped through my leggings as I breathed in the fresh air, savoring the early morning sunshine on my face. By the time I reached the shoreline, my coffee mug was empty. I stood beside a rock, staring out over the water at the mountains in the distance.

Home.

I watched the sun lift into the sky and catch the ripples on the water before I turned, ready to head home. But a tiny bark stopped me.

A ball of yellow fluff came bounding down the path,

giving another yip. His tail wagged as he tried to slow, but he skidded on the gravel and crashed straight into my legs.

His own legs were wet and his paws muddy as he jumped and pounced around my ankles.

I laughed, bending down to pet his little head, getting licked in the process. "Hey, buddy. You are cute."

"Rocket," came a voice down the road.

A man jogged my direction with a red leash in his hand.

"I'm so sorry." He rushed to the dog, clipping the leash onto a matching collar. "We're working on stay. And come. And heel. It's not going well."

I laughed and stood, shielding my eyes from the glare. When his face came into view, my breath caught. *Oh, wow.*

His face was disarming. As striking as the sunrise at my back. His dark hair was messy and finger-combed away from his face. Flecks of caramel and gold danced in his brown eyes. Broad shoulders filled out his sweatshirt. Faded jeans draped down long legs.

"Thanks for catching Rocket," he said.

"No problem." My cheeks flushed. Great voice too. Deep and rugged.

He held out his hand and flashed me an easy smile that made my heart skip.

Time stopped.

"I'm Mason Drummond."

acknowledgments

Thank you for reading Timeless!

A special thanks to my editing and proofreading team: Elizabeth Nover, Julie Deaton and Judy Zweifel. Thank you to Sarah Hansen for the stunning cover. And Stacey Blake for the gorgeous paperback formatting.

The Lark Cove series was originally going to be three books before I added Tinsel. That was it. Four books. But in the back of my mind, Aubrey and Landon's story was always a possibility. It just hadn't worked in my calendar. Until this past year, when my family took a trip to the real-life town that inspired Lark Cove, and I was hit with this rush of nostalgia. And I just had to go back. To every reader who has picked up these books in the past four years, thank you. I am so incredibly grateful for you all. These stories have held a special place in my heart. And I hope they've stayed in yours too.

about the author

Devney is a *Wall Street Journal* and *USA Today* bestselling author who lives in Washington with her husband and two sons. Born and raised in Montana, she loves writing books set in her treasured home state. After working in the technology industry for nearly a decade, she abandoned conference calls and project schedules to enjoy a slower pace at home with her family. Writing one book, let alone many, was not something she ever expected to do. But now that she's discovered her true passion for writing romance, she has no plans to ever stop.

Don't miss out on Devney's latest book news.

Subscribe to her newsletter!

WWW.DEVNEYPERRY.COM

other titles

Jamison Valley Series

The Coppersmith Farmhouse

The Clover Chapel

The Lucky Heart

The Outpost

The Bitterroot Inn

The Candle Palace

Maysen Jar Series

The Birthday List

Letters to Molly

Lark Cove Series

Tattered

Timid

Tragic

Tinsel

Timeless

Clifton Forge Series

Steel King

Riven Knight

Stone Princess

Noble Prince

Fallen Jester

Tin Queen

Runaway Series

Runaway Road

Wild Highway

Quarter Miles

Forsaken Trail

Dotted Lines

The Edens Series

Christmas in Quincy - Prequel

Indigo Ridge

Juniper Hill

Garnet Flats

Jasper Vale

Crimson River

Sable Peak

Preview to Indigo Ridge

INDIGO RIDGE

Enjoy this preview to *Indigo Ridge*,
book one in the Edens series.

WINSLOW

"Could I get another . . ."

The bartender didn't slow as he passed by.

"Drink," I muttered, slumping forward.

Pops had told me that this bar was where the locals hung out. Not only was it within walking distance of my new house in case I decided not to drive, but I was a local now. As of today, I lived in Quincy, Montana.

I'd told the bartender as much when I'd asked for his wine list. He'd raised one bushy white eyebrow above his narrowed gaze, and I'd abandoned my thirst for a glass of cabernet, ordering a vodka tonic instead. It had zapped every ounce of my willpower not to request a lemon twist.

The ice cubes in my glass clinked together as I swirled around my pink plastic straw. The bartender ignored that sound too.

Main Street had two bars—tourist traps this time of year, according to Pops. But I regretted not choosing one of those to celebrate my first night in Quincy. Given his attitude, the bartender, who must have thought I was a lost tourist, regretted my decision too.

Willie's was a dive bar and not exactly my scene.

The bartenders downtown probably acknowledged

their customers, and the prices were listed on a menu, not delivered using three fingers on one wrinkled hand.

He looked about as old as this dark, dingy building. Like most small-town Montana bars, the walls were teeming with beer signs and neon lights. Shelves stacked with liquor bottles lined the mirrored wall across from my seat. The room was cluttered with tables, every chair empty.

Willie's was all but deserted this Sunday night at nine o'clock.

The locals must know of a better place to unwind.

The only other patron was a man sitting at the farthest end of the bar, in the last stool down the line. He'd come in ten minutes after I'd arrived and chosen the seat as far from me as possible. He and the bartender were nearly carbon copies of one another, with the same white hair and scraggly beards.

Twins? They looked old enough to have established this bar. Maybe one of them was Willie himself.

The bartender caught me staring.

I smiled and rattled the ice in my glass.

His mouth pursed in a thin line but he made me another drink. And like with the first, he delivered it without a word, holding up the same three fingers.

I twisted to reach into my purse, fishing out another five because clearly starting a tab was out of the question. But before I could pull the bill from my wallet, a deep, rugged voice caressed the room.

"Hey, Willie."

"Griffin." The bartender nodded.

So he was Willie. And he could speak.

"Usual?" Willie asked.

"Yep." The man with the incredible voice, Griffin, pulled out the stool two down from mine.

As his tall, broad body eased into the seat, a whiff of his scent carried my way. Leather and wind and spice filled my nose, chasing away the musty air from the bar. It was heady and alluring.

He was the type of man who turned a woman's head.

One glimpse at his profile and the cocktail in front of me was unnecessary. Instead, I drank this man in head to toe.

The sleeves of his black T-shirt stretched around his honed biceps and molded to the planes of his shoulders as he leaned his elbows on the bar. His brown hair was finger-combed and curled at the nape of his neck. His tan forearms were dusted with the same dark hair and a vein ran over the corded muscle beneath.

Even seated, I could tell his legs were long, his thighs thick like the evergreen tree trunks from the forests outside of town. Frayed hems of his faded jeans brushed against his black cowboy boots. And as he shifted in his seat, I caught the glimmer of a silver and gold belt buckle at his waist.

If his voice, his scent and that chiseled jaw hadn't been enough to make my mouth go dry, that buckle would have done it.

One of my mom's favorite movies had been *Legends of the Fall.* She'd let me watch it at sixteen and we'd cried together. Whenever I missed her, I'd put it on. The DVD was scratched and the clasp on the case was broken because I'd watched that movie countless times simply because it had been hers.

She'd always swooned over Brad Pitt as a sexy cowboy.

If she could see Griffin, she'd be drooling too. Though he was missing the hat and the horse, this guy was every cowboy fantasy come to life.

Lifting my glass to my mouth, I sipped the cold drink and tore my gaze from the handsome stranger. The vodka burned my throat and the alcohol rushed to my head. Ol' Willie mixed his cocktails strong.

I was unabashedly staring. It was rude and obvious. Yet when I set the glass down, my gaze immediately returned to Griffin.

His piercing blue eyes were waiting.

My breath hitched.

Willie set down a tumbler full of ice and caramel liquid in front of Griffin, then, without giving him the fingers to pay, walked away.

Griffin took a single swallow of his drink, his Adam's apple bobbing. Then his attention was on me once more.

The intensity of his gaze was as intoxicating as my cocktail.

He stared without hesitation. He stared with bold

desire. His gaze raked down my black tank top to the ripped jeans I'd put on this morning before checking out of my hotel in Bozeman.

I'd spent four and a half hours driving to Quincy with a U-Haul trailer hitched to my Dodge Durango. When I'd arrived, I'd immediately jumped into unloading, only breaking to meet Pops for dinner.

I was a mess after a day of hauling boxes. My hair was in a ponytail and whatever makeup I'd put on this morning had likely worn off. Yet the appreciation in Griffin's gaze sent a wave of desire rushing to my core.

"Hi," I blurted. *Smooth, Winn.*

His eyes twinkled like two perfect sapphires set behind long, sooty lashes. "Hi."

"I'm Winn." I held out a hand over the space between us.

"Griffin." The moment his warm, calloused palm grazed mine, tingles cascaded across my skin like fireworks. A shiver rolled down my spine.

Holy hell. There was enough electricity between us to power the jukebox in the corner.

I focused on my drink, gulping more than sipping. The ice did nothing to cool me down. When was the last time I'd been this attracted to a man? Years. It had been years. Even then, it paled in comparison to five minutes beside Griffin.

"Where are you from?" he asked. Like Willie, he must have assumed I was a tourist too.

"Bozeman."

He nodded. "I went to college at Montana State."

"Go Bobcats." I lifted my drink in a salute.

Griffin returned the gesture, then put the rim of his glass to his full lower lip.

I was staring again, unashamed. Maybe it was the angular cheekbones that set his face apart. Maybe it was the straight nose with a slight bump at the bridge. Or his dark, bold browbone. He was no ordinary, handsome man. Griffin was drop-dead gorgeous.

And if he was at Willie's . . . a local.

Local meant off-limits. *Damn.*

I swallowed my disappointment with another gulp of vodka.

The scrape of stool legs rang through the room as he moved to take the seat beside mine. His arms returned to the bar, his drink between them as he leaned forward. He sat so close, his body so large, that the heat from his skin seeped into mine.

"Winn. I like that name."

"Thanks." My full name was Winslow but very few people ever called me anything other than Winn or Winnie.

Willie walked by and narrowed his eyes at the sliver of space between Griffin and me. Then he joined his doppelganger.

"Are they related?" I asked, dropping my voice.

"Willie Senior is on our side of the bar. His son is mixing drinks."

"Father and son. Huh. I thought twins. Does Willie Senior have the same glowing personality as Willie Junior?"

"It's worse." Griffin chuckled. "Every time I come through town, he gets crankier."

Wait. Did that mean . . . "You don't live in town?"

"No." He shook his head, picking up his drink.

I did the same, hiding my smile in the glass. So he wasn't a local. Which meant flirting was harmless. *Bless you, Quincy.*

A hundred personal questions raced through my mind, but I dismissed them all. Skyler used to criticize me for going into interrogation mode within ten minutes of meeting someone new. One of many critiques. He'd used his profession as a life coach as an excuse to tell me anything and everything I'd been doing wrong in our relationship. In life.

Meanwhile, he'd betrayed me, so I wasn't listening to Skyler's voice anymore.

But I still wasn't going to bombard this man with questions. He didn't live here, and I'd save my questions for the people who did: my constituents.

Griffin looked to the far end of the room and the empty shuffleboard table. "Want to play a game?"

"Um . . . sure? I've never played before."

"It's easy." He slid off his stool, moving with a grace that men his size didn't normally possess.

I followed, eyes glued to the best ass I had ever seen. And he didn't live here. An imaginary choir perched in the bar's dusty rafters gave a collective *yeehaw*.

Griffin went to one end of the table while I walked to the other. "Okay, Winn. Loser buys the next round of drinks."

Good thing I had cash. "Okay."

Griffin spent the next ten minutes explaining the rules and demonstrating how to slide the pucks down the sand-dusted surface toward the point lines. Then we played, game after game. After one more round, we both stopped drinking, but neither of us made a move to leave.

I won some games. I lost most. And when Willie finally announced that he was closing at one, the two of us walked outside to the darkened parking lot.

A dusty black truck was parked beside my Durango.

"That was fun."

"It was." I smiled up at Griffin, my cheeks pinching. I hadn't had this much fun openly flirting with a man in, well . . . ever. I slowed my steps because the last place I wanted to go was home alone.

He must have had the same idea because his boots stopped on the pavement. He inched closer.

Winslow Covington didn't have one-night stands. I'd been too busy wasting years on the wrong man. Griffin wasn't the right man either, but I'd learned in my time as a cop that sometimes it wasn't about choosing right from wrong. It was choosing the *right* wrongs.

Griffin. Tonight, I chose Griffin.

So I closed the distance between us and stood on my toes, letting my hands snake up his hard, flat stomach.

He was tall, standing two or three inches over six feet. At five nine, it was refreshing to be around a man who towered over me. I lifted a hand to his neck, pulling him down until his mouth hovered over mine.

"Is that your truck?"

~

"Shit." I cursed at the clock, then flew into action, flinging the covers off my naked body and racing for the bathroom.

Late was not how I wanted to start the first day of my new job.

I flipped on the shower, my head pounding as I stepped under the cold spray and let out a yelp. There was no time to wait for hot water, so I shampooed my hair and put in some conditioner while I scrubbed Griffin's scent off my skin. I'd mourn the loss of it later.

There was an ache between my legs that I'd think about later too. Last night had been . . .

Mind blowing. Toe curling. The best night I'd ever had with a man. Griffin knew exactly how to use that powerful body of his and I'd been the lucky recipient of three—or had it been four?—orgasms.

I shuddered and realized the water was hot. "Damn it."

Shoving thoughts of Griffin out of my head, I hurried out of the shower, frantically swiping on makeup and willing the blow dryer to work faster. Without time to curl or straighten my hair, I twisted it into a tight bun at the nape of my neck, then dashed to the bedroom to get dressed.

The mattress rested on the floor, the sheets and blankets rumpled and strewn everywhere. Thankfully, before I'd headed to the bar last night, I'd searched for bedding in the boxes and laid it out. When I'd finally gotten home after hours spent in the back of Griffin's truck, I'd practically face-planted into my pillows and forgotten to set my alarm.

I refused to regret Griffin. Kicking off my new life in Quincy with a hot and wild night seemed a little bit like fate.

Serendipity.

Maybe on his next trip through town, we'd bump into each other. But if not, well . . . I didn't have time for the distraction of a man.

Especially not today.

"Oh, God. Please don't let me be late." I rifled through a suitcase, finding a pair of dark-wash jeans.

Pops had told me specifically not to show up at the station looking fancy.

The jeans were slightly wrinkled but there was no

time to find whatever box had stolen my iron. Besides, an iron meant fancy. The simple white tee I found next was also wrinkled, so I dug for my favorite black blazer to hide the worst offenders. Then I hopped into my favorite black boots with the chunky heels before jogging for the door, swiping up my purse from where I'd dumped it on the living room floor.

The sun was shining. The air was clean. The sky was blue. And I had no time to appreciate a minute of my first Quincy, Montana, morning as I ran to the Durango parked in my driveway.

I slid behind the wheel, started the engine and cursed again at the clock on the dash. *Eight-oh-two.* "I'm late."

Thankfully, Quincy wasn't Bozeman and the drive from one side of town to the police station on the other took exactly six minutes. I pulled into the lot and parked next to a familiar blue Bronco and let myself take a single deep breath.

I can do this job.

Then I got out of my car and walked to the station's front door, hoping with every step I looked okay.

One disdaining look from the officer stationed behind a glass partition at the front desk and I knew I'd gotten it wrong. *Shit.*

His gray hair was cut short, high and tight in a military style. He looked me up and down, the wrinkles on his face deepening with a scowl. That glare likely had nothing to do with my outfit.

And everything to do with my last name.

"Good morning." I plastered on a bright smile, crossing the small lobby to his workspace. "I'm Winslow Covington."

"The new chief. I know," he muttered.

My smile didn't falter.

I'd win them over. Eventually. That's what I'd told Pops last night when he'd had me over for dinner after I'd returned the U-Haul. I'd win them all over, one by one.

Most people were bound to think that the only reason I'd gotten the job as the Quincy chief of police was because my grandfather was the mayor. Yes, he would be my boss. But there wasn't a nepotism clause for city employees. Probably because in a town this size, everyone was likely related in some manner. If you added too many restrictions, no one would be able to get a job.

Besides, Pops hadn't hired me. He could have, but instead, he'd put together a search committee so that there'd be more than one voice in the decision. Walter Covington was the fairest, most honorable man I'd ever known.

And granddaughter or not, what mattered was my performance. He'd take the cues from the community, and though my grandfather loved me completely, he wouldn't hesitate to fire me if I screwed this up.

He'd told me as much the day he'd hired me. He'd reminded me again last night.

"The mayor is waiting in your office," the officer

said, pushing the button to buzz me into the door beside his cubicle.

"It was nice to meet you"—I glanced at the silver nameplate on his black uniform—"Officer Smith."

His response was to ignore me completely, turning his attention to his computer screen. I'd have to win him over another day. Or maybe he'd be open to an early retirement.

I pushed through the door that led into the heart of the station. I'd been here twice, both times during the interview process. But it was different now as I walked through the bullpen no longer a guest. This was my bullpen. The officers looking up from their desks were under my charge.

My stomach clenched.

Staying up all night having sex with a stranger probably hadn't been the smartest way to prepare for my first day.

"Winnie." Pops came out of what would be my office, his hand extended. He seemed taller today, probably because he was dressed in nice jeans and a starched shirt instead of the ratty T-shirt, baggy jeans and suspenders I'd seen him in yesterday.

Pops was fit for his seventy-one years and though his hair was a thick silver, his six-three frame was as strong as an ox. He was in better shape than most men my age, let alone his.

I shook his hand, glad that he hadn't tried to hug me. "Morning. Sorry I'm late."

"I just got here myself." He leaned in closer and dropped his voice. "You doing okay?"

"Nervous," I whispered.

He gave me a small smile. "You'll do great."

I could do this job.

I was thirty years old. Two decades below the median age of a person in this position. Four decades younger than my predecessor had been when he'd retired.

The former chief of police had worked in Quincy for his entire career, moving up the ranks and acting as chief for as long as I'd been alive. But that was why Pops had wanted me in this position. He said Quincy needed fresh eyes and younger blood. The town was growing, and with it, their problems. The old ways weren't cutting it.

The department needed to embrace technology and new processes. When the former chief had announced his retirement, Pops had encouraged me to toss my name into the hat. By some miracle, the hiring committee had chosen me.

Yes, I was young, but I met the minimum qualifications. I'd worked for ten years with the Bozeman Police Department. During that time, I'd earned my bachelor's degree and a position as detective within their department. My record was impeccable, and I'd never left a case unclosed.

Maybe my welcome would have been warmer if I

were a man, but that had never scared me and it certainly wasn't going to today.

I can do this job.

I would do this job.

"Let me introduce you to Janice." He nodded for me to follow him into my office, where we spent the morning with Janice, my new assistant.

She'd worked for the former chief for fifteen years, and the longer she spoke, the more I fell in love with her. Janice had spiky gray hair and the cutest pair of red-framed glasses I'd ever seen. She knew the ins and outs of the station, the schedules and the shortcomings.

As we ended our initial meeting, I made a mental note to bring her flowers because without Janice, I'd likely fall flat on my face. We toured the station, meeting the officers not out on patrol.

Officer Smith, who was rarely sent into the field because he preferred the desk, had been one of the candidates for chief, and Janice told me that he'd been a grumpy asshole since the day he'd been rejected.

Every officer besides him had been polite and professional, though reserved. No doubt they weren't sure what to make of me, but today I'd won Janice over—or maybe she'd won me. I was calling it a victory.

"You'll meet most of the department this afternoon at shift change," she told me when we retreated back to the safety of my office.

"I was planning on staying late one evening this week to meet the night shift too."

This wasn't a large station, because Quincy wasn't a large town, but in total, I had fifteen officers, four dispatchers, two administrators and a Janice.

"Tomorrow, the county sheriff is coming in to meet you," Janice said, reading from the notebook she'd had with her all morning. "Ten o'clock. His staff is twice the size of ours but he has more ground to cover. For the most part, their team stays out of our way, but he's always willing to step in if you need help."

"Good to know." I wouldn't mind having a resource to bounce ideas off of either.

"How's your head?" Pops asked.

I put my hands by my ears and made the sound of an exploding bomb.

He laughed. "You'll catch on."

"Yes, you will," Janice said.

"Thank you for everything," I told her. "I'm really looking forward to working with you."

She sat a little straighter. "Likewise."

"Okay, Winnie." Pops slapped his hands on his knees. "Let's go grab some lunch. Then I've got to get to my own office, and I'll let you come back here and settle in."

"I'll be here when you get back." Janice squeezed my arm as we shuffled out of my office.

Pops simply nodded, maintaining his distance. Tonight, when I wasn't Chief Covington and he wasn't

Mayor Covington, I'd head to his house and get one of his bear hugs.

"How about we eat at The Eloise?" he suggested as we made our way outside.

"The hotel?"

He nodded. "It would be good for you to spend some time there. Get to know the Edens."

The Edens. Quincy's founding family.

Pops had promised that the fastest way to earn favor with the community was to win over the Edens. One of their relatives from generations past had founded the town and the family had been the community's cornerstone ever since.

"They own the hotel, remember?" he asked.

"I remember. I just didn't realize there was a restaurant in the hotel these days." Probably because I hadn't spent much time in Quincy lately.

The six trips I'd taken here to participate in the interview process had been my first trips to Quincy in years. Five, to be exact.

But when Skyler and I had fallen to pieces and Pops had pitched the job as chief, I'd decided it was time for a change. And Quincy, well . . . Quincy had always held a special place in my heart.

"The Edens started the hotel's restaurant about four years ago," Pops said. "It's the best place in town, in my opinion."

"Then let's eat." I unlocked my car. "Meet you there."

I followed his Bronco from the station to Main Street, taking in the plethora of out-of-state cars parked downtown. Tourist season was in full swing and nearly every space was full.

Pops parked two blocks away from Main on a side street, and side by side, we strolled to The Eloise Inn.

The town's iconic hotel was the tallest building in Quincy, standing proudly against the mountain backdrop in the distance. I'd always wanted to spend a night at The Eloise. Maybe one day I'd book myself a room, just for fun.

The lobby smelled of lemons and rosemary. The front desk was an island in the grand, open space, and a young woman with a sweet face stood behind the counter, checking in a guest. When she spotted Pops, she tossed him a wink.

"Who's that?" I asked.

"Eloise Eden. She took over as manager this past winter."

Pops waved at her, then walked past the front desk toward an open doorway. The clatter of forks on plates and the dull murmur of conversation greeted me as we entered the hotel's restaurant.

The dining room was spacious and the ceilings as tall as those in the lobby. It was the perfect place for entertaining. Almost a ballroom but filled with tables of varying sizes, it also worked well as a restaurant.

"They just put in those windows." Pops pointed at

the far wall where black-paned windows cut into a red-brick wall. "Last time I talked to Harrison, he said this fall they'll be remodeling this whole space."

Harrison Eden. The family's patriarch. He'd been on the hiring committee, and I liked to believe I'd made a good impression. According to Pops, if I hadn't, there was no way I'd have gotten my job.

A hostess greeted us with a wide smile and led us to a square table in the center of the room.

"Which of the Edens runs the restaurant?" I asked as we browsed the menu card.

"Knox. He's Harrison and Anne's second oldest son. Eloise is their youngest daughter."

Harrison and Anne, the parents. Knox, a son. Eloise, a daughter. There were likely many more Edens to meet.

Down Main, the Eden name was splashed on numerous storefronts, including the coffee shop I wished I'd had time to stop by this morning. Last night's antics were catching up to me, and I hid a yawn with my menu.

"They're good people," Pops said. "You've met Harrison. Anne's a sweetheart. Their opinion carries a lot of weight around here. So does Griffin's."

Griffin. *Did he say Griffin?*

My stomach dropped.

No. This couldn't be happening. It had to be a mistake. There had to be another Griffin, one who didn't live in Quincy. I'd specifically asked him last night if he lived in town and he'd said no. Hadn't he?

"Hey, Covie."

So busy having my mental freak-out that I'd slept with not only a local man, but one I needed to see me as a professional and not a backseat hookup, I didn't notice the two men standing beside our table until it was too late.

Harrison Eden smiled.

Griffin, who was just as handsome as he had been last night, did not.

Had he known who I was last night? Had that been some sort of test or trick? Doubtful. He looked as surprised to see me as I was to see him.

"Hey, Harrison." Pops stood to shake his hand, then waved at me. "You remember my granddaughter, Winslow."

"Of course." Harrison took my hand as I stood, shaking it with a firm grip. "Welcome. We're glad to have you as our new chief of police."

"Thank you." My voice was surprisingly steady considering my heart was attempting to dive out of my chest and hide under the table. "I'm glad to be here."

"Would you like to join us?" Pops offered, nodding to the empty chairs at our table.

"No," Griffin said at the same time his father said, "We'd love to."

Neither Pops nor Harrison seemed to notice the tension rolling off Griffin's body as they took their chairs, leaving Griffin and me to introduce ourselves.

I swallowed hard, then extended a hand. "Hello."

That sharp jaw I'd traced with my tongue last night clenched so tight that I heard the crack of his molars. He glared at my hand before capturing it in his large palm. "Griffin."

Griffin Eden.

My one-night stand.

So much for serendipity.